CW01073084

The Fortune Teller

Also by Alison Prince

Dear Del
Bird Boy

The Fortune Teller

ALISON PRINCE

Hodder
Children's
Books

a division of Hodder Headline

Copyright © 2001 Alison Prince

First published in Great Britain in 2001
by Hodder Children's Books

The right of Alison Prince to be identified as the Author of
the Work has been asserted by her in accordance with
the Copyright, Designs and Patents Act 1988.

10 9 8 7 6 5 4 3 2

All rights reserved. No part of this publication may be reproduced,
stored in a retrieval system, or transmitted, in any form or by any
means without the prior written permission of the publisher, nor be
otherwise circulated in any form of binding or cover other than that
in which it is published and without a similar condition being
imposed on the subsequent purchaser.

All characters in this publication are fictitious and any resemblance
to real persons, living or dead, is purely coincidental.

A catalogue record for this book is available from
the British Library

ISBN 0340 80568 4

Typeset by Avon Dataset Ltd, Bidford-on-Avon, Warks

Printed and bound in Great Britain by
Clays Ltd, St Ives plc

Hodder Children's Books
A Division of Hodder Headline Ltd
338 Euston Road
London NW1 3BH

One

Mick Finn walked along the harbour wall towards
the lighthouse. It was past nine in the evening
but the sun still shone across the sea and the
sandstone parapet felt warm under his hand
from the day's heat. Rusty ran ahead, stopping
sometimes for a sniff and a piddle, the way dogs
did. *Not that there's much for him to sniff at*, Mick
thought. Most people walked their dogs along the
beach, not up here on a high wall that didn't go
anywhere. *Don't know why I do it*.

The lighthouse wasn't much to look at. It stood
at the end of the wall to warn ships of the narrow
entry into the harbour, and it wasn't very tall. Not
one of those huge things built on some isolated
rock, just a stumpy tower with thick glass windows
all round and an iron gate that kept everyone out
except the maintenance men.

He was too early. Mick always hoped he'd be
there to see the lighthouse give out its first beam

1

of the evening – that would be magic. But he'd never managed to time it right. Tonight was no good, of course. It was early June, getting on for midsummer when the nights hardly got properly dark at all. The lighthouse wouldn't start working for another hour, probably. He turned to go back.

The wall divided the sea from the car park below Mick on his left. There were a good few cars there tonight, lined up in tidy rows. People taking the ferry across to Broray tended to leave their cars here rather than ship them. Not surprising, considering what the ferry company charged, Mick thought. Everyone was grumbling about it. They grumbled about the car park, too, because the cars got vandalised. There was talk of putting up a fence and security lights, but it probably wouldn't happen – hardly worth it when they were going to withdraw the Northern Irish ferry. There were plans to shift it to a different terminal with wider access to its harbour, and that would just leave the Broray line, busy in the summer but half empty through the winter months.

It had been a winter night when Mick's dad drove into the car park and had his argument with the wall. He'd come off second best. Mick stopped and stared down. He didn't always stop.

Mostly, he wasn't thinking about it and he just walked past. After all, it happened six years ago, long enough to put it behind him. He'd only been eight at the time, and Kate was ten. No point in thinking about it. But sometimes the questions came back.

What had his father been doing down there in the middle of the night? Showing off his handbrake turns, perhaps – he was always a flashy driver. Mick shrugged and walked on. The police had made enquiries of course, but all Bob's mates swore blind they'd been at home in bed. *Just as well*, Mick thought. *If you're going to die, make a good mystery of it*. Bob always had style.

Rusty had sat down to wait patiently, but when Mick moved on he got up and ran ahead of him. They went down the steps from the wall and across the car park, skirting the dock with its high fence where lorry containers waited to be shipped to Belfast. Mick whistled the dog to heel as they came to the road and the buildings. He crossed the single-line railway that ran out to the harbour and turned the corner past the pub. After that there was the sea-front with its wide stretch of grass, and houses standing back on the far side of the road. The town used to be quite busy once. Even now, there were still geraniums in the flowerbeds, but they hadn't been dead-headed, and weeds grew among the brown remains of the blossoms, not to mention the Coke cans and beer bottles people chucked there. Loops of cable that held coloured light-bulbs still hung between the lamp-posts but since the Council stopped switching them on, the kids had been throwing stones at them.

It hadn't always been like this, Mick thought. Dad used to call it a Victorian gem. He had plans to turn The Laurels into the kind of guesthouse people came to year after year. He and Cathie were going to get the place up to Tourist Board standard then into the West of Scotland guide book. Maybe even Egon Ronay. No harm in aiming high.

Only it hadn't happened. Mick walked on past the crazy golf that had a dumped supermarket trolley among its concrete humps and hollows, and stopped to look at The Laurels across the road. He could see why they didn't get many visitors now. *I must do something about the bushes*, he thought. *Cathie can't cope with them.* He liked to think of his mother as Cathie – it made him feel more grown up. Maybe he'd tackle the bushes when the school holidays started. He'd had a shot at it once or twice before, but they'd gone past what you could do with secateurs. It was more like a chain-saw job.

Rusty was having a tail-waving conversation with a West Highland terrier belonging to an elderly lady. Mick whistled, but he took no notice.

'Such a lovely evening, isn't it!' the lady said happily as Mick approached. 'We're having a beautiful summer.'

'Yes, great.' Mick knew who she was. She lived in a boarding house three doors down, one of their permanent residents. *Absolute gold-dust*, he thought. The Laurels would be sunk without their two.

'And what's your doggie's name?' the lady enquired.

'Rusty.' *Doggie. Yuk.*

'That's nice. Because of his colour, I suppose.'

'Yes. We left him out in the rain when he was a pup.'

'Oh, poor wee soul.'

'Um – joke,' said Mick. *Talk about dim.* 'We love him, really. Come on, Rusty.'

He crossed the road and turned into the drive between its empty gateposts. Bob had said he was going to get wrought-iron gates. The house was covered with ivy. It was quite a pretty sort, with yellow centres to its leaves, but it had caused endless trouble, growing in through the windows and blocking up the gutters so the rain ran down the walls. A couple of years ago, it had pushed the telephone junction box off the wall, and no one could make any calls. Cathie had got a couple of blokes in to cut it back.

What a pair they'd been, Mick thought. 'You've slates off your roof, Missus,' they'd said. 'And rot in your window frames.' They wanted money in advance, to buy materials, they said, but they'd spent half their time in the pub. And at the end of it, rain was coming in through new places and plaster was falling off the ceilings. Cathie made them patch up the worst of it, but since then it had been one thing after another, and there was never any money to put it right.

He went on up the drive and through the back door into the kitchen. His mother looked up from stacking the dishwasher and said, 'Hi, love. Nice walk?'

'Fine.' Cathie seemed a bit ratty, Mick thought. He could guess why. 'Is Kate out?'

'Is she ever in,' said Cathie. 'But she's sixteen, isn't she. Nothing I can do about it.'

'Well, there you go,' said Mick. It was one of those meaningless Scottish phrases that didn't say anything, but when Cathie got started it didn't

6

matter much whatever you said.

'Why did she have to pick Jake?' she was asking. 'He's years older than her. And he doesn't have a proper job or anything.'

'He plays the saxophone,' said Mick.

'That's not a job. And don't tell me he gets his share of the gig money, I know. Kate keeps saying. But he could use some of it to get his hair cut. He'll never get a job looking like that.'

Mick thought Jake was OK. 'There aren't any jobs, really,' he said mildly. 'Only the bacon factory.'

'There's nothing the matter with the bacon factory. I know a lot of people who work there.'

'The *people* are all right.' But Mick had seen the pigs being unloaded from their lorry, trotting so obediently down the ramp, and the thought of what happened to them made him feel a bit queasy, even though he liked bacon. 'It's just the place,' he said. 'I wouldn't want to work there.'

'Then you'll have to get your exams, won't you. Go on to uni, get a degree. If I'd done that, I wouldn't be stuck here.'

Mick had heard it all before, but he tried to be encouraging. 'Come on, Mum, you never know what's going to happen. Something may crop up.' It seemed a good line of argument. 'After all,' he went on, 'when you were at school you didn't know you were going to marry Dad and come here. You could have done anything. You still could.'

'Fat chance.'

'No, honest. You don't know what's waiting for you in the future.'

'Probably just as well,' Cathie said.

Mick went over to the kettle and weighed it in his hand to see how much water was in it. 'Cup of tea?'

Cathie sighed. 'Yes, love, that would be great.' She came over and put her arms round him, needing a hug. 'Whatever would I do without you?' she said.

Mick wished she wouldn't hug him – he was getting too old for that. They'd had this kind of conversation a thousand times, and it nearly always ended the same way. *What would I do without you.* And Mick didn't know what she'd do. He was taller than her now, he could pick her up off her feet. He frowned to himself. *If I do go to college, how will she cope?*

The kettle boiled. Mick made two mugs of tea and carried them into the little sitting room where Cathie was already curled on the sofa with her shoes off, flicking through channels on the TV. That was always the handy answer, he thought. It didn't matter what they ended up watching, it saved them from any more talk. He handed his mother her tea and sat down beside her. *Whatever would we do without it.*

Two

On his way home from school the next day, Mick stopped at Mr Khan's shop with Neil and Danny and a few others, and they shared a couple of KitKats and kicked a Coke can around on the pavement until Mr Khan came out and said they were making the place look untidy.

Mick went on home after that, and got in at about ten to five, which wasn't unusually late – and his mother burst into tears.

'*Mickey!*' she said (she always called him Mickey). 'Oh, thank God!' And she clung to him with a grip like an octopus and cried all over his shoulder.

'Mum, what's the matter?' he asked when he could disentangle himself. 'What's happened?'

She shook her head and turned away. 'It's nothing.' But her voice was wobbly. 'Just being silly,' she managed to add. 'Got worried, waiting for you.'

'Look, I'm fourteen,' said Mick. 'I'm quite good at crossing roads now.'

She didn't smile, just said, 'I know.'

Mick tried again. 'I'm not much later than usual anyway, I don't see why you're upset.'

Cathie wiped her eyes and then gave her head a small shake. She wasn't going to tell him.

'Mum – come on, what is it?' Mick was starting to feel alarmed. Cathie always told him everything. Even the time when a drunk had tried to kiss her in the Post Office, she'd told him all about it in detail. *'He smelt so vile, Mickey, you can't imagine.'* So what could have happened that was too awful to talk about? 'You've got to tell me,' he said. 'What is it?'

Her red-rimmed eyes gave him a scared glance then slid away. 'I just got the heebies,' she said. 'On my own too much, I expect.' She reached up to ruffle his hair. 'Don't look so worried.' Then her face crumpled and she was weeping again.

Mick put his arms round her and rocked her gently. 'Come on,' he said, as he would to a child who had fallen over and hurt herself. 'It's all right.' But it obviously wasn't. A frightening thought struck him, and for a moment he couldn't move. 'You're not ill, are you?' Had she come from the doctor with terrible news? Cancer?

11

A death sentence? *Please God, no.*

Cathie managed to smile through her tears. 'Oh, Mickey, you're so sweet. Fancy thinking of that.' She wiped her eyes again. 'No, love, I'm all right. Just – tired, I suppose.' She sat down at the kitchen table and leaned her head on her hand.

The kettle was hot. Mick switched it on to boil again and made two mugs of tea. He never much liked the smell of it when the boiling water first hit the teabag, but that was all part of the ritual. Life in the Finn household went from one tea-making to another, like a soap opera starting and ending with its signature tune.

Cathie took a sip or two then said, 'I've always felt worried about you, ever since you were born. You nearly died when you were a baby.'

'I know,' Mick said. 'You told me.' *Dozens of times.* Something to do with him being the wrong way up inside her. So embarrassing. 'I'm all right now, though.'

To his relief, Kate came clattering down the stairs that led to the family bedrooms. Guests used the posh ones at the front of the house. She was dressed for going out. Black trousers, bare midriff, big hoop earrings. With her black hair and her level, dark eyes she looked older than sixteen. She had her denim jacket over her shoulders and carried the rucksack she used for her school books. Pausing behind Cathie, she caught Mick's eye and made a face, then said, 'You OK now, Mum?'

'I'm fine,' said Cathie stiffly. Kate had never had much patience. If things got at all heavy, she just went out.

'I might not be back,' said Kate. 'Jake's lot are playing at the Caledonia Club, but they're on the late spot.' She paused and added, 'You couldn't let me have some money, could you?'

Cathie sighed, reaching for her handbag.

'I'll pay you back, honest,' said Kate. 'I'm getting a job at the Drop In Centre. Jake fixed it for me. Assistant cook.'

Cathie looked up, shocked out of whatever was troubling her. 'What about school?'

'I've left,' said Kate. She took the note Cathie was holding out and stuffed it into her trouser pocket. 'Thanks a lot. See you.' She glanced at Mick with an affectionate wrinkling of her nose, then was gone.

When Mick took Rusty for his evening walk, Cathie insisted on coming too. She seemed jumpy, grabbing at his sleeve as they waited to cross the road. Mick couldn't think what had got into her. But at least she'd stopped crying.

It was just as bad the next day, and the one after that. Cathie treated Mick as if he was a toddler again, begging him to be careful of the traffic and warning him not to talk to strangers and be sure to come straight home.

On Friday morning Kate lost her temper. 'For goodness' sake, Mum, will you stop trying to wrap him in cotton wool!' she exploded. Cathie had just taken the bread knife out of Mick's hand in case he cut himself. 'It's totally sick-making!' She grabbed her bit of toast and her rucksack and went out, slamming the door. She was spending every day at the Centre now, though her job didn't officially start until Monday.

'She doesn't understand,' said Cathie.

'Nor do I,' said Mick. 'Whatever's going on, I wish it wasn't.'

His mother put her hand over her eyes and shook her head. 'You can't help, love,' she said. 'Nobody can.'

And that made it even worse.

Since the next day was a Saturday, Mick spent the

morning hanging round the house and trying to make himself useful, hoping this would cheer his mother up a bit, but she still seemed to be locked in a private anxiety. Lunchtime came and went. Mick took Rusty for a walk, but Cathie insisted that Kate should go with him. 'I don't like you being out alone,' she said.

'What on earth's the matter with her?' Kate said as they walked across the green. 'She seems to be totally off her head – this obsession with safety.'

'Perhaps she's heard about someone else's son having an accident,' said Mick.

'Could be, I suppose.' Kate thought about it. 'But things have happened before and she wasn't upset. Remember when Janice McCafferty fell off her bike in front of that bus? Mum thought it was awful – I mean, we all did – but she wasn't that bothered.'

'We didn't have bikes,' said Mick.

While they ate a silent tea, Mick mentally rehearsed ways of reminding his mother that he was going ten-pin bowling with Neil and Danny tonight. It was Neil's birthday treat, and his dad was taking them – but Mick had a feeling Cathie wasn't going to like it.

He was right. 'Oh, Mickey, don't!' she begged him. 'There was a fight outside that place last week, and a boy got knifed.'

Kate rolled her eyes and groaned, and Mick said, 'It was just a gang thing – nothing to do with anyone else. And Neil's dad's coming with us. I told you. You said it was all right.'

Jake came in through the kitchen door, tall and untidy in a faded T-shirt and dilapidated jeans. 'Hi,' he said easily, and sat down on the sofa.

'I won't be long,' said Kate. 'I'll just go and change.' But she lingered, because Cathie was still trying to persuade Mick to stay at home.

'It's just asking for trouble,' she was saying. 'Nobody can be watching all the time, you just don't know what's going to happen.'

Mick began to feel irritated. 'Look, Mum, I'll be perfectly all right. You don't have to panic.' He'd almost called her Cathie, but he couldn't quite do that. Not yet.

'I'm not panicking. I just want to keep you safe, that's all.'

'There's no such thing as safety,' Jake said, and Cathie rounded on him in fury.

'Oh, thank you very much! I suppose that's the sort of rubbish they dish out at your horrible

Centre, is it? All this Buddhist stuff about going with the flow. Well, you can just keep it to yourself.'

'They're not Buddhists,' Jake said mildly. 'What's the matter, anyway?'

'Mind your own business.' She was close to tears again.

'Second thoughts, I won't bother changing,' Kate said to Jake. 'Let's get out of here, OK?'

Jake shrugged. 'Whatever,' he said, and got to his feet.

Kate looked at Cathie. 'Take it easy, Mum. Things are all right, honest.'

Cathie didn't answer, and after a few moments Kate gave up. She raised her eyebrows at Mick and said, 'Have a good time. See you later.' Then she and Jake went out.

Mick retreated to his room and put his best jeans on, and a clean shirt. When he came down, Cathie was sitting in front of the TV. She didn't take her eyes from it as she said, 'What time will you be back?'

'Half-past ten,' Mick promised, then wished he hadn't.

He was in by twenty to eleven, having turned down an invitation to go back to Neil's house for pizza, and Cathie was still sitting there as if she hadn't moved.

'I've walked the dog,' she said. 'You don't have to go out again.'

'Oh.' Mick liked his evening walk with Rusty. 'All right, then.' He hovered uneasily for another few moments, but she didn't say anything else. He gave a little cough and said, 'I'll go to bed, then.'

'Yes.' Her eyes met his unhappily, but she managed a smile. 'Goodnight, love.'

'Night.'

Sunday was worse. Cathie vacuumed and dusted in silence, and Kate hadn't reappeared from wherever she went last night. Mick did more homework than he'd done for months, up in his room. At lunchtime Cathie said she wasn't hungry. She looked white-faced and anxious, and Mick began to wonder if she'd been lying to him when she said she wasn't ill. He made himself a sandwich and ate it, then said he'd take Rusty out. 'And you don't have to come, Mum – just have a rest. You look really tired.'

'But where are you going, Mickey?'

'Up to the Castle, probably.'

She pressed her lips together in a kind of flinch.

'Do watch where you're going, won't you? It's very steep up there.'

For Pete's sake, Mick thought – but he managed not to say anything. He grabbed Rusty's lead from the hook by the kitchen door, whistled for the dog and went.

It was a huge relief to be out of the house. The sky was open and sunny, and the straight line of the sea was as calm as ever, unmoved by any outbreaks of human panic. It didn't know a boy called Michael Finn existed, let alone why his mother was so frantic about keeping him safe.

Michael, Mick, Mickey. He could take his pick what he called himself. Mickey was the worst option – a stupid joke, really. Mick remembered how his dad used to laugh and punch him gently on the shoulder. 'My knock-out kid,' he'd say. It was years before Mick found out that a Mickey Finn was the knock-out stuff a gangster might put in your drink. *Very funny, Dad, thanks a lot*. And Cathie still went along with it, as if it would be disloyal to Bob if she called Mick by any name other than the one his father had used.

A narrow road between the houses led to the footbridge over the railway. Mick climbed up its steps and crossed over. On the other side, a path to the right led down to the Council houses on the low ground by the railway, but the hill ahead of him was the way up to the Castle. As soon as he let Rusty off the lead the dog shot ahead, barking excitedly in the hope of seeing rabbits. *Fat chance with all that row*, Mick thought – but at that precise moment he caught a glimpse of a small grey shape bolting for shelter under some bushes.

There was a lot of chasing around after that, Rusty scrabbling madly at rabbit holes in the short turf then charging off again with Mick after him. When he was thoroughly out of breath and Rusty's nose and front paws were covered with earth, Mick sat down on the grass with his back against a sun-warmed bit of ruined wall, and stared out across the sea. You could see a lot of it from up here. It sparkled in the afternoon sun, and the outline of Broray was plain on the horizon. When it was wet or misty the island disappeared, and some people said it wasn't an island at all, just a cardboard cut-out that was there sometimes and sometimes not. Funny how they kept on cracking the same old joke. The sun was dazzling, and Mick closed his eyes. He felt the untidy thump as Rusty lay down beside him, panting.

It's good up here, he thought. No talking and

anxiety, no guests to whom one must be polite. No blocked drains and draughty windows and leaky roofs, no frantic mother. This hill had been the same for thousands of years. Even before the Castle was built and fell down again, the rock beneath it had been here. The thought had never occurred to him before in all the times he'd been up here, and he wondered idly why he was thinking it now. Perhaps he needed to.

He stayed there all afternoon, but then the heat of the day began to pass, and Mick thought uneasily of his mother. She would be worrying. He put his arms round his knees and frowned as the usual thoughts started to creep back. Why couldn't Cathie be in charge of her own worries? He cared about her – of course he did – but sometimes it felt as if her troubles spread themselves around like germs, to make other people feel bad as well. But he couldn't blame her. *Poor Mum, it's not her fault.* He sighed, and Rusty raised his head and looked at him.

'Better go,' said Mick.

Kate was in when he got back. She was peeling potatoes at the sink, and when Mick came in she gave him a very deliberate wink, followed by a roll of the eyes towards Cathie, who was frying onions.

Mick raised his eyebrows, and Kate nodded. *So she's found out what the trouble is,* he thought.

With her back to both of them, Cathie wiped her eyes with the back of her wrist, either because of the onions or something else. Mick went over and said, 'You all right?' and she nodded – though she obviously wasn't. He fed Rusty then went upstairs.

Kate called him down for tea – beefburgers, onions and chips – and while they ate she chattered on about Jake's band and what the last two gigs had been like, and about starting work at the Centre tomorrow. Mick talked as well, but Cathie hardly said anything, and she didn't eat much, either. Mick caught her looking at him sometimes, but if he met her eye she looked away. When they'd finished, he said he had homework to do. It wasn't true because he'd already done it in the morning, but it gave him an excuse to escape to his room again.

After a bit, Kate slipped in and closed the door behind her.

'Listen, Mick, I've got to tell you this,' she said. 'I found out what's the matter with Mum – but it's pretty weird. She went to see a fortune teller.'

'You're kidding,' said Mick. *All this fuss because of something as stupid as that?*

'No, honest.' Kate looked at him with a trace of concern. 'You mustn't get this wrong, it's just a load of rubbish – but the woman said you were going to die.'

For a moment, Mick felt as if the meal he had eaten was lurching uneasily in his stomach. 'Oh, great,' he said.

Kate rushed on. 'She's got to be off her head, of course. I mean, fancy telling anyone a thing like that.'

'When?' asked Mick.

'When what?'

'When am I going to – die?' It was quite hard to say that short word.

'Not till you're ancient,' Kate said firmly. 'Look, you mustn't start taking this seriously, or you'll be as bad as Mum. She's frantic, of course.'

'I've noticed.' *No wonder*.

'I could wring the woman's neck,' said Kate. 'What is she on, some power trip or something? Totally crackers. Somebody ought to go and sort her out.'

Mick nodded. *But Dad died*, he thought. *In the middle of being so alive*. Freaky accidents could happen to anyone. Look at Danny's aunt, driving her car along the esplanade when a roosting bat flew out from under the dash, scared her so much she hit a lamp-post. The insurance wouldn't believe it. She wasn't killed, but . . .

'Come on,' said Kate, giving Mick's shoulder a little shake. 'Don't look so worried.'

'All right for you.' What about Tracey Burns in the third year, who died of leukaemia?

'The woman doesn't *know*,' Kate insisted. 'Nobody does. I only told you so you'd understand what's up with Mum. The whole thing's a load of tosh. You're as safe now as you ever were.'

'Yes,' Mick agreed. But a huge question hung in the air, and he dared not voice it. *How safe is that?*

Three

Mick didn't say anything to Cathie about the fortune teller that evening. They all sat and watched TV in silence. He wondered if Kate was going to say she'd told him, but she didn't. *Not surprising really*, he thought. Kate wouldn't want to get involved in an emotional scene.

At about ten, Cathie took the dog out, giving no reasons.

'You'll have to tell her,' said Kate.

'I know. I'll do it tomorrow.' Then Mick added, 'How did you make her say what was the matter?'

'Just got mad with her. I said if she didn't tell me the reason, I'd assume she was a paranoid schizophrenic.' Kate had picked up a lot of psychological words through spending so much time at the Centre.

'What does that mean?'

'You think the whole outside world is against you.'

Mick nodded. *For some people*, he thought, *it really could be*.

In the morning, he got through a bowl of cornflakes in the usual hurry. *No time to talk about it now*. But as he grabbed his school bag and made for the door he relented and looked back at his mother, who was gazing at him in mute unhappiness.

'You mustn't worry,' he said. 'I'll be all right.' And mentally crossed his fingers. *I hope*.

'Oh, Mickey – did Kate tell you?'

'Yes. Can't stop now. See you this evening. OK?'

She nodded but her lips were trembling. 'Take care,' she managed to say.

At the edge of the empty road that ran by the green, Mick stopped and looked both ways. He hadn't thought about it before, but of course, bad luck could fall on you in countless different ways. There'd been something on TV about a bus driver who had a heart attack at the wheel and ploughed into a queue of people. And in Glasgow last week a chunk of masonry had fallen off a building and just missed a woman and her dog. He paused again at the single-track railway, although he knew the train never came past unless the lights were flashing. All the same, it had managed to hit a van three years ago.

He walked on to Union Street, then jumped half out of his skin when a car hooted at a truck that had turned without any signal. *It's like being in a horror movie*, he thought, *waiting for something awful to happen.* All he needed was the creepy music.

School was a bit better. It didn't seem likely that disaster could strike when they were all sitting in classrooms, doing the usual things. Then in Woodwork Kevin Roberts ran a chisel through his hand. Clean through, from the palm to the back. There wasn't much blood but it looked gruesome, sticking out a clear centimetre. Mr McKelvie packed him off to hospital, chisel and all, then lectured the class at some length on stupidity and carelessness.

Mick's thoughts were galloping about like frightened rabbits. Maybe a fortune teller would have known this was the day for Kevin to have an accident. He was a slow, careful boy, not the sort who mucked about, but that wasn't the point. The accident could have been there in advance, lined up and waiting for him to have it.

Danny put his hand up and said he didn't think Kevin had been careless – the chisel had just slipped, that was all.

'Then he was guilty of bad workshop practice,' Mr McKelvie said severely. 'How often have I told you to make sure your hands are behind your work, not in front?'

Teachers hated accidents, Mick thought, in case someone said it was their fault. That was why Mr McKelvie was insisting that Kevin himself was to blame – but he didn't have much support from the class. Most people thought accidents just happened. Jamie Paterson said a woman at the bacon factory broke her hip when a dead pig fell on her. He knew, because his mother worked there. 'And that wasn't anyone's fault,' he said.

'Yes, it was,' Mr McKelvie retorted. 'Somebody didn't hang the pig up properly.' But Chloë Johnson, who had opted for Woodwork instead of Home Economics, looked mystic and said perhaps they'd been *meant* not to.

Exactly, Mick thought.

Mr McKelvie nearly blew a fuse. He said he'd never heard such superstitious rubbish, and if that was Chloë's attitude she'd better stick to needlework where she couldn't hurt herself.

Chloë said that was a sexist remark, and Dougie Weston said his sister had sewed right over her thumbnail with a sewing machine, but the bell went before things got any more heated, and they all trooped out to the chip van.

Mick didn't tell anyone about the fortune teller. Bad enough to have a nagging nightmare at the back of his mind without people saying things like, 'Still here, then?' No, this was best kept to himself.

Cathie was upstairs when he got in, showing some visitors to their rooms. He could hear her voice from the upstairs landing, sounding very bright and encouraging. 'Breakfast is from eight to half-past nine, but if you'd like it any earlier it's no trouble.'

We're good at taking trouble, Mick thought. He just hoped they wouldn't notice the missing tiles in the bathroom or the smell of damp in the lounge.

Someone tapped at the kitchen door and Mick opened it to find Miss McIver standing in the hall, clutching her copy of *The Lady* to her Pringle twin-set and looking peeved.

'Ah, Michael,' she said (Miss McIver had no truck with nicknames), 'I just wondered – it's gone half-past four and there seems to be no sign of tea.'

Grumbling old bat, Mick thought. He gave her his professional smile and said, 'Mum's just showing some people to their room, but it won't be a moment. The kettle's on.' It wasn't, but you had to keep the guests happy.

'I see. I'll be in the lounge.' And off she went with her magazine and her leather bag that contained her own personal Sweetex and her perpetual crochet.

Mick fished a paper doyley out of the packet and put it on a plate for the biscuits, and switched the kettle on. Miss McIver never missed a chance to make out she was being neglected, but The Laurels would be sunk without her and Mrs Morris, 'the Ems', as he and Cathie called them. He put the plate of biscuits on a tray and added cups and saucers and the sugar bowl for Mrs Morris, who also took milk. Miss McIver did not. Then Cathie came in, and hugged him wordlessly.

'Miss Em's been moaning about the tea being late,' said Mick.

'I'm sure she has,' said Cathie. She made the tea and put the cosy over the pot.

Mick picked up the tray. 'I'll take it.'

The Ems were sitting in armchairs on either side of the coffee table in the lounge, reading their magazines in reproachful silence – but Mrs Morris could never keep it up for long.

'Tea!' she said. 'How nice. Thank you, Mickey.'

30

Miss McIver gave her a contemptuous glance and turned another page. *For a person who goes to church twice on Sundays*, Mick thought, *she isn't very forgiving*. He left them to it.

The kitchen seemed to be bursting with unspoken words. Mick didn't know where to start. 'Are the new people staying long?' he asked.

'Only two days. Down here for an eightieth birthday, so they'll be round there for meals.'

'Pity.' There was more money in it if guests ate at The Laurels.

Cathie had made them a couple of mugs of tea. Mick sat down at the table and watched his hand stirring the brown liquid. Then he heard himself say, 'It doesn't change anything, Mum. Just because someone says something – it doesn't have to be true.' His words weren't making much sense, but Cathie nodded.

'That's what I keep telling myself. Only – it might be.'

'I know.' *I must do better than this*, Mick told himself. But he couldn't seem to find a really good, convincing argument.

'It's such a nightmare,' Cathie said. 'Sometimes I almost forget about it, then it all comes back again and I'm just sick with fear.'

Mick nodded. He knew how she felt. 'But what did she actually say, Mum? How did she do it? Did she read your hand or what?'

'It was cards. Tarot cards, not the ordinary sort. They all had pictures – really weird.'

'What was the woman like? Where does she live?'

'In a flat over the betting shop in Union Street. She's quite old. You can see her hair's white, but she dyes it orange, and she's got this wrinkled skin. Black eyes, though, jet black. I couldn't look away.'

'How did you find her? Did someone tell you?'

Cathie shook her head. 'She's got a postcard advert on the board in Mr Khan's shop. Your Future Revealed.'

'What's her name?'

'Verity Rose. I don't suppose it's her real name. There used to be a Gypsy Rose Lee, and Verity means Truth.'

'Is she a gypsy?' Mick had a vision of gold earrings and fringed shawls.

'I don't think so,' said Cathie. 'The flat's quite ordinary. Small sitting room with a brown and yellow carpet, rather hideous. Electric fire, two armchairs and a sofa. She had one of those bubble things on the mantelpiece.'

'Bubble things? D'you mean a lava lamp?'

'I don't know – a tall jar with oil in it and a light underneath and these big bubbles going up and down. Turquoise blue, hers was. I've seen them pink as well, or orange. She'd only just finished her lunch,' Cathie added. 'The things were still on the table, she had to clear them so she could lay the cards out. I hadn't phoned or anything, just rang the bell on impulse.'

'So what about these cards? How many were there?'

'Oh, lots.' Cathie's hands were linked round her mug and she stared into it unseeingly, trying to remember. 'She picked one out on purpose first, and laid it face up – the Queen of something, I forget what. She said that stood for me. A dark-haired woman.'

'She wasn't fooled by the streaks, then?' Mick said. His mother had been so horrified to find a white hair or two appearing that she'd rushed off to the hairdresser and got it streaked with what she called silver. Dead smart, even if it did make her look a bit like a zebra.

'No,' said Cathie, not smiling.

'So what next?'

'She said it would be a Celtic Cross layout. She dealt another card from the pack on top of mine.

I remember that one – it was the Five of Cups. The cups were lying on their sides all higgledy-piggledy and it meant my luck was running out.'

'Oh, great,' said Mick. 'Then what?'

'She laid one crosswise. I forget what it was, but she said it meant I was burdened with responsibilities. Then she put out four more, one on each side of the crossed cards. There was one that meant I was looking back to a happier time, then there was the Queen of Cups.'

'So what was that about?'

'It meant I was the victim of circumstances. Then there was one about money worries, and one that said I was looking back to a happier time. Honest, Mickey, it was so right, it was uncanny.'

It didn't sound too awful up to now, Mick thought. 'So was that the lot?'

'Oh, no,' said Cathie. 'She filled in the whole circle then laid groups of four cards down the sides.' Unconsciously she pushed the mug aside and folded her arms, her hands gripping her elbows as though she was seated at that other table. 'There was one called The Hanged Man. Not hanged by his neck – he was upside down, dangling by one foot. She said he was free of the earth and all its troubles because a sacrifice had been made.'

Mick swallowed uneasily. 'Go on.'

Cathie smiled in an embarrassed way. 'There was one called The Lovers. She said I was going to meet someone who'd change my life.'

'That would be good,' said Mick, trying to sound encouraging.

His mother sighed and sat back. 'To be honest, I've sometimes wished I could meet someone,' she said. 'I mean, you're great, love, but you won't always be here.' Then her hand flew to her mouth and she gave a small gasp, realising what she'd said.

'I'll be off to college or something,' Mick said quickly.

'Yes, exactly.' Then she shrugged. 'But fortune tellers always go on about the tall, handsome stranger, don't they. I'm not believing *that*.'

'Then you can't believe any of it,' Mick pointed out. 'You either think she can see the future or you don't. You can't pick and choose.'

Cathie stared at him. 'You're right,' she said. Then her eyes slid away. 'I don't know. I want to write it all off as nonsense, but I daren't. I mean, what if something does happen to you? Some stupid thing I could have prevented? I'd feel so terrible if I'd been warned and I chose to take no notice.'

Mick could see her point. But the cards still didn't sound as if his life had really been threatened. 'What else was there?' *May as well know the worst.*

'There was The Sun. That seemed quite good.' Then she ducked her head, running her fingers through her silver-streaked hair. 'The worst came in the last four. What she called The Final Outcome. Death. And one that meant the broken-hearted mother. And The Star,' she added, struggling not to cry, 'for hope.'

'Oh, big deal,' said Mick. Then he had an idea. 'Look, Mum, if she'd put all the cards back in a pile and shuffled them then dealt them out again, you'd have got a different fortune.'

'I know,' Cathie said. 'I asked her if we could do that, and she said it was best not to. It only makes you feel worse if the same cards come up again. And if they don't, and you just get a random mix, then what's the point? You've just muddied the water, you're not getting a message at all. And the same cards *do* tend to come back,' Cathie added. 'I used to notice it when I played whist.'

'I never knew you played whist,' said Mick.

36

'My mother liked it. We used to go to whist drives in the church hall. I was still at school.'

'Weird.'

For a confusing moment, Mick had a vision of Cathie as a dark-haired girl walking through the streets of Ayr beside her mother, who was now Mick's gran. And Gran didn't know him at all, or Cathie either, because she was in a home with Alzheimer's, frowning at the chocolates they brought her as if she'd never seen such a thing before. He suddenly saw how helpless everyone was, being carried along by time like dead pigs on a line. His mouth was dry as he asked the next question. 'This thing about me – did she say when it would happen?'

Cathie's lips trembled, and she struggled for self-control. 'She thought it would be soon,' she said. 'This autumn. By the end of September, if not before.' And she put her hand over his and held it as if she would never let him go.

Four

At that moment, Kate and Jake came in. Kate flopped into a chair and said, 'I'm shattered.'

'I thought you might find it tiring,' said Cathie, releasing Mick's hand, and Mick asked, 'How did it go?'

'OK,' said Kate. 'There's not much actual cooking except for making a couple of pots of soup. Just microwaving spuds and making filled rolls and things. I think it's the people who are tiring. Most of them are fine, but there's some who can't decide what they want – and there's one or two who don't really talk at all.'

'So what's the matter with them?' Cathie asked.

'They're unhappy,' Jake said. Everyone looked at him, and Mick remembered that Jake himself had been in hospital because of what he called 'the miseries.'

'What are they unhappy about?' enquired Kate.

Jake shrugged. 'I expect they think the world is

awful. And it is, mostly. You just have to get used to it. Anyone want a Coke?' He offered the large bottle he was carrying.

'No, thanks,' said Cathie. Mick put his hand out and Jake passed him the bottle. He unscrewed the cap and took a swig, then offered it to Kate, who shook her head.

'Are you both staying for supper?' asked Cathie.

'If that's OK,' said Jake. 'I'll get a take-away if you like – I've got some money.'

'There's no need – I'm doing spaghetti.'

'The Ems don't like spaghetti,' Mick reminded his mother. 'At least, Miss Em doesn't.'

'I know. They can have pies from the freezer.' She got up from the table. 'Mickey, would you do some spuds for me? There's a dear.'

'And mind you don't cut yourself,' Kate said.

Cathie's face went tight and she said, 'I don't think that's very funny.'

'Oh, come on,' said Kate. 'Lighten up. You can't really believe all that tosh.'

'It's not a question of believing it,' Cathie said. 'But it makes sense to be on the safe side. And don't give me any of your lectures,' she added to Jake.

'Mum!' Kate protested.

'Well.' And Cathie went off to get the Ems' tea tray from the lounge.

'Honestly, what is she like,' said Kate.

But nobody answered.

The next morning, Mick got up in time to give Cathie a hand, seeing there were extra people in the house who might want a cooked breakfast. He laid their table with the usual stuff then added a bottle of tomato ketchup, just in case. The Ems never had anything fried. Miss McIver had half a grapefruit and two slices of brown toast with margarine and lime marmalade, though she switched to porridge in the winter. And it had to be served with a small jug of cream that had stood in the fridge all night. Mrs Morris just had a lot of coffee, and some cornflakes if she was up to it. She was usually a bit hung over in the mornings, due to her fondness for a wee nip of whisky, taken in the privacy of her room. She smuggled the empties out to the bottle-bank in a fancy bag that had LIBRARY BOOKS embroidered on it.

The dining room was always a bit dim in the mornings despite its tall windows, because the sun didn't work its way round until later. Mick had switched the wall lights on, but they suddenly went out. He heard his mother emerge from the kitchen and open the door of the cupboard where the fuse box was.

'What's happened?' he asked. They got power cuts sometimes when it was windy, but this was a fine, sunny morning.

'Don't know.' He knew she'd be standing on a chair in there, peering around with a torch. Not that she knew anything about electricity. He heard switches being clicked off then on again. 'Nothing's working,' she said.

'Just as well we've got gas for cooking,' said Mick. He went into the kitchen and put a saucepan of water on to boil. Sounds of complaint were coming from upstairs, and doors were being banged.

'That'll be the Ems,' said Cathie. 'The shower won't be working, and there's no light in the loos. Blast.' She picked up the phone and dialled. Miss McIver came downstairs in her dressing gown and slippers, looking deeply offended.

'Yes, I *know*,' Cathie told her, listening to the phone. 'The power's off. I'm dealing with it as fast as I can.'

'I see. Is there—'

Cathie held up her hand, listening to a recorded message. 'Oh, *rats*,' she said, and put the phone down. 'He's on holiday,' she told Mick. '*Now* what do I do?'

'I was going to say, is there any hope of a candle?' Miss Em continued.

'I'll get you one,' said Mick, grabbing a torch to rummage in the cupboard.

Armed with her candlestick and a box of matches, Miss McIver retreated upstairs, looking like Lady Macbeth on a bad day. Cathie was thumbing through the phone book. She dialled again.

'Is that Mr Macbain? Oh, good. It's Cathie Finn, from The Laurels guesthouse. All our power's gone off. I phoned Andy Paterson who usually comes, but he's on holiday till next week . . . Could you really? That would be brilliant. You know where we are? . . . Great. See you soon, then.'

'Coming?' asked Mick.

'Yes, at about ten. He's got something to do first, but he said it shouldn't take long. You'd better light the grill if you want toast,' she added. Mick had absent-mindedly dropped two slices of bread into the electric toaster.

Mick thumped himself on the forehead for being an idiot and fished the slices out again. 'What's the time?' he asked. The wall clock had stopped.

Cathie looked at her watch. 'Gone half-past

eight. You'd better be off. Shall I make that into a sandwich for you?'

'I'll do it.' He was already taking the lid off the peanut butter jar. He added some Marmite, crammed the slices together and took a bite. 'See you,' he added indistinctly, and grabbed his bag.

'Sure.' But her face was anxious again, and he paused.

'Don't worry,' he said. 'I'll be careful.'

And she nodded.

Nothing dangerous happened all day, and when Mick got home, the fridge was purring and the hand on the kitchen clock was turning again. Cathie came into the kitchen followed by a stoutish, dumpy man with sticking-out ears, holding a toolbox. She smiled when she saw Mick. 'All working again,' she said.

'That's good,' said Mick.

'We need to replace the fuse box.'

'Sounds expensive,' Mick said – but his mother didn't seem too concerned. She switched on the kettle and turned to the electrician. 'Tea, Mr Macbain? Or would you prefer coffee?'

'Coffee would be great.' He pulled out the chair she indicated and sat down at the table. 'Everyone calls me Donald,' he added. 'And as to the cost –'

his rather small blue eyes looked at Mick – 'I'm doing your mum a reasonable deal. There's a few wee jobs needing done round the place. Cheaper to get them all sorted while I'm at it.'

Mick was doubtful. The guys who cut the ivy back had said the same thing, and look what a mess they'd made.

'We don't have much choice,' Cathie told him. 'Apparently our system is totally out of date. The Health and Safety would close us down if they saw it Mr Macbain says. Donald.'

'Old-fashioned wire fuses,' said the electrician. 'See, you get no protection to your equipment with those. You need a cut-out at the board.'

Mick shrugged. He'd take the man's word for it. There was no point in arguing with Cathie, anyway. If she thought the place was likely to burn down, she'd be desperate to make it safe. He listened idly as she and the electrician chatted. His mother sounded much more Ayrshire when she was talking to Donald Macbain. When Mick and Kate were kids she'd always been rather severe if they sounded too Scottish. People who wanted to get on in life had to sound well-spoken, she said. And Bob, of course, hadn't been Scottish at all. He was from a place called Chipping Sodbury. Cathie sometimes said Mick's voice reminded her of him.

'I'll be round in the morning,' Donald Macbain was saying. 'Say about ten? After you've given your people their breakfast and got cleared up – I'll need to have the power off.'

'That would be great,' said Cathie. 'Heavens, when I think how dangerous it must have been . . .' She was careful not to look at Mick, but he knew what she meant.

The electrician turned up as promised. When Mick came home from school the next day, he found Cathie standing in the cupboard, gazing with admiration at the new fuse box, which certainly looked very neat and business-like.

'There's no actual fuses, just a row of wee switches, look!' she said. 'And Donald's put a light in here so I don't need a torch. Isn't it good!'

'Each one's labelled so you know where the trouble is,' said Donald. 'And they trip before it shorts back to the plug on the appliance. Cuts out any risk of damage or fire.' He was repacking tools into their metal box. 'I'll do your spotlights tomorrow.'

'There's only one of the spotlights not working,'

said Mick. 'And it mostly comes on if you poke it with a wooden spoon.'

Donald closed the toolbox and stood up. 'Let me show you something,' he said. He led the way back to the kitchen and picked up the dismantled spotlight that was lying on the table. 'See here?' He pushed with his thumb at the brown plastic part that was supposed to hold the bulb, and a lot of crumbly bits fell off it. 'That's supposed to be your insulation,' he said. 'Once it starts to break up, there's nothing to stop these two wires touching.'

'Then you get a short,' said Mick, wanting to show he wasn't a total idiot.

'Exactly.'

'My husband put them in,' said Cathie. 'He liked the idea of directing light wherever you wanted it. Only they are a bit fiddly. Changing a bulb, you've to undo the wee nut at the back, and getting it screwed up again is really awkward.'

'No need to do that with the new ones,' said Donald. 'They take screw-in bulbs. And they've ventilation holes so they don't get so hot – you'll find the bulbs last longer.'

'But the others are all right, aren't they?' Mick asked. No point in spending money if you didn't have to.

'They're all in the same state,' Donald told him. 'These things are pretty cheap these days – under a fiver apiece with trade discount. But it's up to you, of course.'

'No, they'll have to be replaced,' said Cathie. 'Now I know they're dodgy, I'd be worrying all the time.'

'I'll get them tomorrow.' Donald picked up his toolbox. 'You'll be all right to use the existing ones tonight – I've taped over the wires, nothing's going to burst into flames. See you in the morning.' And he went out to his van.

Cathie sighed contentedly. 'So nice to have someone really honest for a change,' she said.

'Yes,' said Mick. He wondered why he felt uneasy. Donald Macbain did seem to be absolutely honest, and very helpful. But Mick couldn't dispel a strange feeling of wariness.

Five

Donald plastered the gaps round the new spotlights which were a slightly different shape from the old ones, and painted them over so they didn't show. 'Making good,' he called it. Mick was reluctantly impressed. Most of the people who had done work at The Laurels shoved off as soon as the job was somewhere near finished, leaving Cathie to bung up the rest with Polyfilla. If anything, they made bad rather than good.

A whole lot of other small jobs followed. Donald put a new exterior light outside the back door – the old one hadn't worked for years – and he cemented the bathroom tiles back in place. He fixed the flashers on Cathie's car. He diagnosed the cause of the damp smell in the dining room as blocked-up air bricks, and dug the earth away outside to expose them, then cut out a bit of rotten skirting board and replaced it.

Cathie seemed confused, Mick thought. She

was pleased about all the improvements in the house, but she couldn't let herself be too pleased because of her fear about the thing that might still happen to Mick. It was like a constant headache for both of them, worse at some times than others.

Mick had a sharp stab of unease when Debbie Jackson's little brother nearly killed himself by pulling the iron off the ironing board. Debbie's mum had just turned aside to put a freshly-ironed shirt on a hanger when wee Ian grabbed at the flex and brought the whole thing down on his head. It knocked him silly and burned his ear and the side of his face, and he was kept in hospital overnight.

'Mum feels terrible,' Debbie said. 'She only took her eye off him for a couple of seconds, but she says it was all her fault.'

'It wasn't,' said Mick.

Debbie looked surprised. 'What d'you mean?'

He shrugged. 'You can't stop an accident from happening if it's going to.' And it was as if the unknown thing that threatened him smiled in agreement.

Neil said, 'I don't think that's right. If someone's got too many things to do all at the same time, like Deb's mum had, then you can't attend to everything. I'm not saying it was her fault, but it could have been different. Maybe she was in too much of a hurry or something. But she was in charge. There didn't have to be an accident.'

'That's what she says,' Debbie agreed.

Mick didn't say any more, but his thoughts followed a path of awful logic. Being in charge could all be written in, like someone writes the script for a TV programme. The hot iron, the hurry, the quick turn aside *and the freedom to do it some other way* were all part of the scenario.

The next lesson picked up on his thoughts as if something out there was amused by his interest. It was Religious Studies, and Miss O'Dell was talking about Hinduism. Not that there were any Hindus in Mick's class – Ahmed was the only Asian, and he was Muslim. But then, they'd done Buddhism last week, and there weren't any Buddhists, either. Miss O'Dell said that wasn't the point.

Today she'd brought in a little bronze statue of Shiva, a god with a lot of arms. He was dancing, with one foot crosswise in the air and the other almost standing on a small baby.

'Poor little thing,' said Chloë Johnson. 'Why's it lying there?'

Miss O'Dell said she mustn't think of it as a real baby. 'It's just a symbol, to show that Shiva is doing the dance of birth and death. People are constantly dying and being born, aren't they? And Hindus believe the soul continues from one life to the next, so dying isn't the end.'

'It means you stop living, though,' Chloë argued.

'Yes, but Hindus say you'll be born again,' Miss O'Dell explained. 'And when you are, your new life will be affected by what you did in the old one. If you were greedy and selfish, you'll have a bad time and everything will be difficult. You might even be born as something not human at all – a toad or a slug. But good, kind people get rewarded and find their lives pleasant and easy.'

'That's just a way of keeping people in line,' said Danny. 'If you thought you were going to come back as a slug you'd watch it, wouldn't you.'

'Well, perhaps,' said Miss O'Dell. 'But anyway, this state of things you're born into is called your karma.' She turned and wrote it on the board. 'It's the way things are for you. The destiny you've earned for yourself.'

Mick closed his eyes in horror. *Look*, he said

silently to the thing that watched him, *if this is about something I did in a previous life, then I'm sorry. But I didn't know, did I?*

Neil put it into words. 'That's not fair,' he objected. 'You can't remember if you were alive before, so why should you be punished for it?'

Chloë agreed. 'Lots of people are poor and starving, but it's not their fault, is it?'

'Just luck,' said Danny.

Miss O'Dell smiled. 'But isn't that why people pray?' she said. 'All religions have the same idea at heart. They all think there's a great spirit – or a lot of spirits – in charge of the way things work. So people pray to be kept safe or to get the things they need and want. There's no point in doing that if you think there's no system and everything happens in a random way. You have to believe that something or someone will hear you and shift the system a little so as to make things better for you. That's what we mean when we talk about faith.' And she wrote FAITH on the board as well.

'My dad's got a system for the Pools,' said Danny, grinning. 'Only it doesn't work.'

'That's because he's not God,' said Chloë.

Danny said, 'He thinks he is.' Everyone was laughing and talking, and Miss O'Dell said loudly,

'Right. Give out these worksheets, Danny, and stop being ridiculous.'

KARMA. FAITH. Mick stared at the two words on the board and swallowed uneasily. For thousands of years, people had believed that something out there really did control your destiny. It wasn't just his imagination.

Walking home, he tripped over a broken paving stone and nearly fell flat on his face.

The sky seemed to be laughing. *Nearly had you.* With slightly worse luck, it could have been some hideous injury. A broken limb that didn't heal, gangrene, blood-poisoning, death. He could have tripped in the road instead of on the pavement, and been run over. Careful, he must be careful.

Mick remembered what Jake had said about flying to Dublin with the band last year. 'I was so scared, I had my bum clenched the whole way. They tell you planes stay in the sky because of their shape and their engines, but I knew better. I was keeping it up there through bum-power.'

Mick wondered if you could stay alive through bum-power. He was suddenly charged with anger as he thought about some god or whatever it was having it in for him. *I don't deserve to die*, he thought. He'd been pretty good, compared with some of the boys he knew. He didn't vandalise cars or do graffiti or pinch stuff from shops. He didn't even send the swings in the play park flying so high that they went over the top and ended up wrapped round the high bar so little kids couldn't use them – and that happened all the time.

He reached the bottom of Union Street then turned left and followed the road round to the broad sweep of grass by the sea. There he flopped down on a seat that had several slats missing and squinted up at the sky. People thought God was up there, didn't they. With angels and all that. Heaven. Someone or something could watch you from the sky, as if you were a goldfish in your own transparent bowl.

Rubbish. The sky was just stuff like any other stuff, only thinner. Gases. Oxygen and nitrogen and something. Carbon dioxide, was it? And radio waves, things like that. Vibrations. *Good Vibrations*. The old Beach Boys tune was back in his mind – it used to be a favourite of Bob's. He used to play the tape in his car.

Mick got up and walked on. He stopped at the kerb and looked both ways, then crossed over to The Laurels. Donald Macbain's van was in the drive again. Mick wondered what he was doing this time; there weren't any more jobs now, unless he was going to decorate the whole place, and Cathie couldn't afford that. He opened the kitchen door – and stopped dead. Cathie and Donald had sat back very quickly, but Mick knew with utter certainty that they'd been holding hands across the table.

'Hallo, love!' Cathie said. 'Had a good day?' But her face was pink, and Donald was studying his empty coffee mug as if it was suddenly very interesting.

The truth hit Mick like a bolt of lightning. Donald was the man the fortune teller had seen in the cards. The man who would change Cathie's life. It was all coming true.

Six

Mick blundered across the kitchen and up the stairs to his room. There was no denying it now. The fortune teller knew what was going to happen.

He lay on his bed and put his hands over his eyes, trying to shut out the thing that waited for him. He was alone with it now. Cathie had someone else to turn to. She'd be all right – she and Donald.

It seemed a long time before his mother tapped at his door and came in. 'Oh, Mickey,' she said, sitting down beside him, 'please don't take it seriously. There's nothing between me and Donald. Honestly.'

Mick almost laughed.

'It was just – I'd been telling him about your dad,' Cathie went on. 'What happened. And he put his hand over mine for a moment because I was upset. He knows what it's like, you see. His wife died of cancer two years ago. But he's just a friend. Nothing more.'

'It's coming true,' Mick said. 'He's changed your life.'

'No!' Cathie's fists were clenched. 'I knew you'd say that. Donald's different, Mickey. He's not some stranger who walked in like a miracle, he's just helpful.'

'But that's the way it works, don't you see?' Mick sat up, almost shouting. 'That's how things have changed. It doesn't have to be drastic, it's just they get a bit easier.'

Cathie pushed her fingers through her hair, staring at him. 'What are we saying? Do I have to live like a prisoner, never seeing anyone in case they turn out to be useful? I had to get the fuse box done, you can see that.'

'Of *course* you did!' Why was she making excuses? The thing was so plain to see. 'That's not the point.' Or perhaps it was, in a way. 'You don't get any choice. Nobody does. The fuse box has got to be replaced, the spotlights turn out to be dangerous, then a whole lot of jobs get done and it's really good, and you end up liking the guy. It's the way it works.'

Cathie shook her head, eyes closed. 'No,' she said. 'No. It can't be.'

Mick didn't answer. *But it is*, he thought.

After a few moments Cathie sighed and let her hands fall in her lap. 'I won't let Donald come here again,' she said. 'You don't have to worry.'

'That won't help,' Mick explained gently. 'You'd just be kidding yourself.' And the waiting thing out there would not be fooled.

When Cathie had gone downstairs, Mick lay back on his bed again, gazing at the ceiling. A few flies were circling under the light in its paper shade, and he watched them idly. Sometimes one of them would speed up and rush through a fast circuit or else dart at another fly and the pair of them would go into a flurry, fighting or mating – something to do with normal fly life. Downstairs, Donald's van started up and drove away.

Mick didn't move. He was aware of the warmth of his feet in their trainers and of breath coming in and out of his lungs. *Dad was alive like this*, he thought. A sudden anger flooded through him and he rolled on his side. Why couldn't Bob have stayed alive? If he was here, Cathie would never have gone to this crackpot fortune teller and she wouldn't be mooning over an electrician with sticking-out ears. The Finns would be a proper family instead of three scared people who kept glancing over their shoulders at fate.

I'm not like that, Kate would say. *It's all rubbish.* She was probably right, Mick thought. He must hang on to that thought, and try to believe it.

There was a scrabbling of paws at the door. Mick got up and let Rusty in before he made a worse mess of the paintwork – Cathie hated him scratching at doors. 'Hallo, you,' he said.

Rusty wagged his tail cheerfully, then jumped on the bed (which was forbidden) and tunnelled about in the crumpled candlewick. Then he rolled on his back with all four paws waving in the air, and whined.

'Oh, all right,' said Mick. 'You want a walk. Come on.' If the Hindus were right about being born again, he thought, he wouldn't mind being a dog.

When he got back, Kate had come in. She was arguing with Cathie in the kitchen. 'I've changed my mind, that's all,' she said.

'But I thought it was settled,' said Cathie. 'Hotel Management is such a sensible thing to study. Once you're qualified, you'll always get a job.'

'I've got a job,' said Kate.

Cathie snorted. 'You can't call microwaving

potatoes in that stupid place a job. You need to go to college, Kate.'

'I know. But I don't want to go yet. I'll think about it later on. I'm not sure about Hotel Management, I might go for something else.'

'That's all very well—'

Mick opened a tin for Rusty and forked the contents into his dish. *Perhaps I won't have to decide what I'm going to do*, he thought. That was one thing to be said for being dead – it let you out of all that careers stuff. If Mick had a free choice, he'd be a vet, but you needed straight As. Some hope.

'I don't expect you to feed me for nothing now I've left school,' Kate was saying. 'I'll pay for my keep while I'm living here.'

'What do you mean, while you're living here? I suppose you're intending to move in with—'

Mick retreated to the sitting room and switched the TV on. Somehow, the question of what Kate was going to do in the future seemed very remote.

Coming home from school the next day was like a re-run of a film he'd seen before. Donald's van was in the drive, and Donald was in the kitchen. Only this time, so was a dumpy, fair-haired girl of about eight, drinking a can of Lilt through a straw.

Donald looked up and said, 'Hi, Mick. This is Sheena. My daughter.'

Cathie was busying herself at the sink. Mick looked at her, willing her to turn round, but she didn't, so he had to look at Sheena instead. 'Hi,' he said.

Sheena released her straw with a glugging noise and said, 'Hi,' then went on sucking. Her hair was pulled back into a ponytail with a scrunchy round it, and she wore a pink T-shirt with kittens on it that was a bit too small.

'Are you the only one?' Mick asked.

Sheena let go of the straw again. 'What d'you mean?'

'Like, do you have brothers or sisters?'

'No, there's just me.'

'We'd have liked a bigger family,' Donald said. 'Only it didn't work out that way.'

His wife had died, Mick remembered. 'Mum told me,' he said. He wondered whether to add that he was sorry. Perhaps not, with Sheena sitting there. He used to hate it when people told him how sorry they were about Bob.

Cathie turned from the sink, drying her hands. 'Tea?'

'Please.'

Her eyes had met his only briefly, but the

glance had told him all he needed to know. She was defiant, helpless, motherly – and very, very afraid.

Seven

At the end of that week, school term ended.

Mick was desperate to get a job. He didn't want to be hanging round the house with Donald popping in the whole time, and he needed to earn some money. But as Jake had once put it, jobs were as rare as rocking-horse shit. Work was like a privilege that some people had and hung on to, and when anyone left a job, there was usually some relative or friend ready to step into it. Mick at fourteen was the bottom of the pile. He tried the bacon factory but they wouldn't have him because he was too young. He didn't tell Cathie he'd been there. If he'd been offered a job he'd have told her of course, but he knew what she'd say. All those knives and machines . . . She'd seen no reason why Jake shouldn't work there, but then Jake wasn't Mick.

Donald was making himself so useful that it was hard to imagine how The Laurels had ever run without him. He mowed the lawn and cut the straggling bushes back with a chain-saw then took the branches away in his van. He raked out all the dried leaves and rubbish that had accumulated underneath and binned that as well. If the phone rang when he was in the house, he'd answer it if Cathie was busy. 'The Laurels – can I help you?' *Anyone would think he owned the place*, Mick thought. There was no question now of Cathie trying to pretend Donald meant nothing to her. She was careful not to make any contact with him when Mick was about, but the pair of them looked at each other far more often than was necessary, as if they found each other strangely interesting. Cathie started taking Donald with her to the Cash and Carry, saying his van was so much handier than her rather clapped-out car – and one day when Mick came in from a fruitless job-hunt he found Donald showing some new guests to their room, because Cathie had gone to get her hair done.

Mick tried to think straight about it. There was no reason why his mother shouldn't find someone new. She'd been on her own for a long time, and Donald was exactly what she needed, even if he did look like a sack of potatoes. Not a bit like Bob, so tall and smiling, with a silk scarf tucked into the neck of his shirt, and a blazer with shiny buttons. *I've got to forget this fortune-teller business*, Mick thought. *Got to.* But when Cathie wasn't looking at Donald her eyes were on Mick with an unchanged sense of strain and anxiety, and she smiled at him in a special, encouraging way, like a dentist who is trying to assure you there's nothing to feel nervous about.

Kate got fed up. It annoyed her that Cathie was cooking proper meals now that Donald was nearly always there, with vegetables served in a dish and chopped mint sprinkled on the potatoes. 'All this fuss,' she said. She spent more and more time round at Jake's, and Mick felt as if everything was shifting. His big sister had gone and Sheena was there instead, and Donald sat where Bob used to, making four at the table again, but a different four. He tried to tell himself it was all right, the sort of thing that happened to dozens of families – and yet he couldn't shake off the feeling that a foreseen destiny was unfolding. And with no way of understanding how such forecasts were made or whether they really meant anything, he was as helpless as a fly tangled in the barely visible silk of a spider's web.

Walking down Union Street the next day after a

fruitless call at a garage reputed to want a petrol attendant (they were looking for someone older) Mick paused out of habit to look in the window of the charity shop. Cathie could never pass it by without going in for what she called 'a rummle around' among the second-hand clothes. She had a real talent for spotting something good, and often came out with a dead smart-looking garment that had only cost fifty pence. Mick thought old clothes were horrible, but he didn't mind having a poke about in the tapes and CDs – not that there were many of those. The shop had old LPs mostly, but Jake still had a turntable, and he was a sucker for jazz records, so it was always worth a look.

There were no CDs at all today, but Mick found a lot of old plastic records in a cardboard box. They were mostly rubbish – opera and stuff – but there was one called Lady Sings the Blues by Billie Holiday. He slid the record out of its sleeve and inspected it for scratches, but it looked all right. And at only ten pence, he wasn't risking much. He tucked the LP under his arm and turned to go to the pay desk – then stopped.

THE TAROT EXPLAINED.

It was just a grubby little paperback with a picture of cards falling from a hand, but his spine prickled. He picked the book up gingerly and opened its pages. The illustrations inside were black and white and very old-fashioned, almost religious-looking. Each one had a Roman number and its name. Mick stared, too disturbed and excited to read the explanations beside each one. There was a woman with her hand over the muzzle of a lion, then a heart pierced by three swords. Not all the cards had numbers – as he turned further, he found the Knight of Pentacles, an armoured man riding a great black horse, holding a five-pointed star in his hand.

Mick had to have the book. It seemed to be almost burning with significance. He closed it with a touch of shivering fear and put it face down with the record, then took both of them to the woman at the pay desk.

'Ten pence your LP,' she said, and turned the book over to see what price was marked inside its jacket. It was blank. 'Where did you find this?'

'It was in the box over there.'

'Ah. Those have only just come in. Margaret!' She called another woman who was putting clothes on hangers. 'How much d'you think for this?'

Margaret came and looked. 'Say five pence – it's only thin.' She glanced at the book again and put it down on the counter rather quickly. 'I wouldn't have it in the house myself,' she said. 'I don't hold with that sort of thing.'

Mick wasn't sure that he held with it, either. More a case of it holding him. The two women were looking at him with disapproval. He handed over fifteen pence and went out with the book and the record in a second-hand plastic bag.

In his room he looked through the brownish pages more carefully, pushing them back into place when they fell away from the cracked glue of the spine. It wasn't an attractive little book, but it might hold the key to the fortune teller's prediction that had laid such a firm grasp on the household. With any luck, it might even prove she was wrong. He turned back and began to read from the beginning.

It was hard going, with a lot of stuff about the Major and Minor Arcana, which meant nothing to him. He ploughed on and came to a section that told him there were four suits in the Minor Arcana, Wands, Cups, Swords and Pentacles. The same idea as spades, hearts, clubs and diamonds in ordinary playing cards, he guessed. Cathie had taught him to play Patience once. Then he came to a bit in italics.

The Tarot consists of symbols. Each card has a deep and complex meaning. The person consulting them must not expect easy answers, for the cards are meant to stimulate the mind in its quest for Eternal Truth.

Mick groaned inwardly. Right now, he'd have settled for an easy answer. Eternal Truth sounded like a slow business. He started looking at the pictures.

Almost at once he came to The Hanged Man. Cathie had talked about that one. The man dangled upside down as she had said, hanging from his left foot that was tied to a bar between two hard-pruned trees with no side branches. His right leg was bent at the knee so his foot lay across the other leg, and his hands were shoved casually in his pockets – or maybe they were behind his back, it was hard to see in the thick black lines of the drawing. Either way, he looked perfectly calm. Mick read the description beside the picture. It ended with ominous words.

His eyes are open as he looks with joy and serenity towards the release of his soul.

Oh, great, thought Mick. *Thanks a lot.* Gooseflesh

was creeping over his skin in spite of the warmth of the day. He couldn't look forward to the release of his soul. He wanted to keep it and go on being alive. The other picture on the same page was even worse. Number XIII, Death, with a picture of a skeleton wielding a scythe. Mick shut the book and rammed it into a drawer, under his socks. This stuff was all right for people who were interested in that kind of thing, people who were feeling OK and wouldn't be upset, but for Mick, the whole thing came too close for comfort.

The rest of the day was a drag. Mick wouldn't have said he actually liked school, but he missed it now, and felt very alone. Neil had gone to Broray with his family because they had relations over there who ran a trekking centre and always needed help in the summer, and Danny was out every day with his dad on his window-cleaning round.

Mick asked Cathie if she'd like him to clean their windows, but she looked doubtful. 'It's really nice of you to ask, love, but don't worry. You're on holiday.' He knew what she left unsaid. *Going up ladders . . . dealing with glass, such dangerous stuff . . .* So he just nodded and wandered off.

Kate didn't come home until late that night. Mick

met her when he came out of the bathroom. 'You all right?' she asked.

'Suppose so.'

'What's the matter?'

He shrugged. 'Wish I could get a job.' He didn't have to explain why.

'I know what you mean,' said Kate. She thought for a moment, then said, 'Look, why don't you come to the Centre? Gavin's always desperate for people who'll help. You won't get paid much, but there's free meals and coffee for anyone on the staff. And it's better than hanging around here.'

Mick went to see Gavin the next day. He looked a bit social-workerish, with a tendency to smile all the time, but he seemed enthusiastic. 'Great,' he said. 'Terrific. Do you think you could paint the railings outside? They're terribly rusty.' He took Mick out and showed him.

The railings were on either side of the stone steps to the front door and ran along in front of the building, which used to be a shipping office years ago. Nobody had painted them for years, and Mick almost smiled. This was a job that would occupy him for days.

He scraped off the loose rust and rubbed the rest down with a wire brush, then Gavin gave him a spray can of stuff to proof the iron against further rusting. It smelt awful, but Mick didn't mind. It was all right out here with the seagulls screaming on the rooftops and people going to and fro. And once he got on to painting the railings with glossy black Hammerite, he began to feel quite pleased with the result.

'Brilliant,' Gavin said when Mick had finished. 'That's smartened the place up no end. You wouldn't like to tackle the toilets, would you?'

'Don't know about *like*,' said Mick, grinning, 'but yes, OK.'

'Good man,' said Gavin.

The toilets were worse than the railings. There were four of them in various parts of the building, and they all had ancient paintwork and flaking plaster and grotty old lino on the floor. Mick scrubbed and sanded and scraped, then filled in the cracks and holes and sanded some more, and Gavin came and looked. 'Great,' he said. 'Really good. Tell you what – just do the walls halfway down with paint and we'll tile the rest. Bit expensive, but once it's done that's it, you don't have to bother again. Harry can help you – he knows all about tiling.'

Harry had dark hair – what was left of it – and a droopy moustache. He was always at the Centre, half-heartedly reading the *Daily Record* or else gazing into space, and Mick had never imagined he could be good at anything. But Gavin was right – when it came to tiling, Harry was an expert. He could cut tiles to fit in the most awkward of spaces, and they never broke in the wrong place like they did when Mick tried it.

'You've to show them who's boss,' Harry said. He scored a tile firmly then tapped it and it fell obediently into two halves. 'No good pussy-footing around.'

'All very well for you,' Mick protested. 'You're brilliant at it.'

'Brilliant.' Harry seemed to like the word. 'Aye, you're right, son. See, I've done some grand places. You know the Commodore Hotel?'

Mick shook his head. 'Is it in Glasgow?'

'No, London. Right in the middle of the posh part. They used to phone up for me, you know, if there was anything special. I've been all over. Exeter, Harrogate, Strathpeffer – they've still got some of the tiles my dad put up in Strathpeffer, just after the First World War. He was in the trade, same as me. London was the best, though. Beautiful toilets at the Commodore. Navy blue for the gents, peach for the ladies. Gold lines round the mirrors and wash-basins. Custom-made tiles, of course, not out of a packet like these.'

'It must have looked amazing,' Mick said politely.

'Amazing, aye, so it was. All gone, though. Two years later, they demolished it.'

'What, the toilet?'

'No, the whole place. Development, they called it. But I know better.' He pressed another tile into place.

'What was it, then?' Mick asked.

'Spies, that's what it was. Industrial espionage. You ever heard of that, Mick?'

'No.'

'When firms steal each other's secrets, stop each other from getting ahead, like nobbling the favourite in a horse race.'

Mick had no idea what he was on about.

'I was too good, you see,' Harry said. 'Couldn't be allowed to go on. When I got back to Glasgow, they sacked me.'

'But why?' The whole story was getting weird.

'That's what they never tell you, son,' said Harry. 'They give you this stuff about overheads and downsizing, but I knew what it meant. I was too good. Showed all the others up. You know something? There's not a toilet of mine left standing, only in Strathpeffer – I reckon they've no' heard about that one. I never worked again.'

'That's awful,' said Mick. But he could see why. If Harry walked into a Job Centre and started ranting about industrial espionage, they were going to write him off as a nutter. Which was a shame, really.

'See, they marked my papers,' Harry went on. '*No job allowed for Harry Baxter*. Official. It was the same everywhere I tried. I've given up now. You can't win, not when they've got the computers and all that. Pass me a tile, son.'

Eight

Mick liked the people at the Centre. He hadn't expected to – he'd thought he would just feel sorry for them. But that wasn't the point. They weren't sorry for themselves, they just thought the ordinary world was ridiculous, or, like Harry, that it was out to get them.

It would be quite easy to feel like that, Mick thought as he painted another toilet. He'd had more than a touch of it himself, walking about like a cat on hot bricks in case sudden death was waiting round the corner. Even now, he was finding it hard to shake off that fear, though the centre seemed comfortable and safe in its ramshackle way. Cathie still didn't like him being out of her sight. She had argued fiercely against him coming to work here, saying he could be putting in some extra schoolwork or just resting and relaxing. Some of the people at the Centre had been through much worse stuff than that, though. They didn't often talk about it, but when someone new arrived, there would be a swapping of experiences and Mick would catch scraps of conversation about mental hospitals where you didn't feel like a person at all, just a walking illness that had to be controlled with drugs or sometimes with physical restraint.

At least at the Centre they are all real people, Mick thought. Some of them were perfectly normal, as far as he could see, though others would keep on telling you the same story, and there were one or two who never spoke at all, like old Beth. She looked a bit like a bag-lady, and she only talked to Gavin's cat, Muggins. He adored her, of course. Mick could see why Beth was very comfortable from a cat's point of view, with all those woollies and cardigans and shawls. Muggins didn't mind that they were held together with safety pins and never got washed. Why should he?

Mick found himself thinking a lot about madness – painting toilets gave you plenty of time to think. It seemed to him that if you wanted people to assume you were sane, you had to say the kinds of thing they expected. Never mind what you really thought, it was better to keep those things private. That's why he hadn't told anyone at school about Verity Rose and her awful prediction. Not because they'd laugh – he could put up with that – but because he didn't think he could pretend well enough that it didn't matter. And once they knew that, they'd look at each other behind his back, and twist their fingers at the side of their heads. *He's a nutter.*

Going home at the end of the day when he'd had his conversation with Harry, Mick heard running footsteps and turned to find Kate catching up with him. She didn't often come back to The Laurels now.

'Hi,' she said, 'how's it going?'

'Great. I really like it there.'

'Oh, good. Gavin's a bit kind of serious, but he tries hard.'

'He's all right.' After a pause, Mick said, 'How do they decide who's a nutter and who isn't?'

'That's what we'd all like to know,' said Kate. 'Jake says it's a sort of confidence thing, like passing a driving test. If they think you can cope and won't damage anyone else, they let you out. Otherwise not.'

Mick thought about it. 'What happens to people in the first place?'

'To get them put in mental hospitals, you mean?' Kate shrugged. 'Could be lots of things.

It's no different from any other illness as far as I can see. Something goes wrong, and you end up just feeling terrible.

Mick hardly liked to ask, but – 'Was that what happened to Jake?'

'Something like that. He doesn't talk about it much. He says the music sorted him out.'

'What, playing the sax?'

'Yes. He didn't have a saxophone then, just a clarinet. He'd learned at school, done his grades and everything, but it was all classical stuff, Mozart and whatnot. Someone else's music, like he says. But there was this guy in the hospital who sang all the time, and it was his own music, out of his head. He only shut up when they sedated him. Jake says that's when he realised he'd always had music in his own head, only he'd never properly heard it. He couldn't wait to get out after that, and start playing it. Not clarinet, though, he wanted a saxophone. Gavin found him one. I don't know how, but he did. Just gave it to him. He didn't want to take any money for it, but Jake gives him some when the band's done a gig, says it's for the Centre. It's up to Gavin what he does with it.'

They walked on. Mick thought of Gavin with new respect. 'What a terrific thing to do,' he said.

'Don't spread it around,' Kate warned. 'He'd be dead embarrassed if everyone knew.'

'Sure.' Mick went on thinking about it as they walked. Maybe Gavin got a kick out of finding something that really did the trick for someone. Most of the time, it wouldn't be so simple. 'What about old Beth?' he said. 'She's funny, isn't she. Never talks to anyone except the cat.'

'She's a bit vague about English,' said Kate. 'She comes from the Western Isles somewhere, so she grew up speaking Gaelic. She fell and broke her hip, and had to move into a home after that, but they wouldn't let her bring her cats. She never quite got over it. Duncan says she has the Sight,' she added.

'Duncan?'

'The skinny old bloke with thick glasses and his trousers tucked into his socks. Does the *Guardian* crossword. He looks a bit weird but he's dead clever. He wrote a book about Second Sight in the Highlands, and he says Beth's got it. She can see into the future.'

'Not another one,' said Mick. He'd had as much future as he could handle.

'I don't mean she tells fortunes. She just kind of knows things.'

They walked on in silence, over the bottom end

of Union Street and past Mr Khan's shop. 'I thought we might ask her about this thing of Mum's,' Kate said as Mick knew she would. 'Whether she thinks it's right.'

Talking to old Beth was not an attractive thought. Snarled-up grey hair, whiskery chin and all those tea-stained cardigans – not to mention the fact that she wouldn't understand a word he said. *And anyway*, Mick thought, *do I want to know?* There was every chance she'd agree with the fortune teller. 'I'd rather not,' he said.

Kate shrugged. 'Fair enough. But I mean, if someone thinks their doctor may have got it wrong, they ask another one, don't they. Second opinion.'

'That's different,' Mick objected. 'Mum and I aren't ill, there's nothing to have an opinion about.'

'I think you are in a way,' said Kate. 'So am I. We're all worried and upset, and that's a kind of illness. We won't shake it off until we've dealt with what's causing it.'

'S'pose so,' said Mick. The truth was, he found old Beth a bit scary. There was something fierce about the pale eyes and the obstinate, wrinkled face. She wasn't a sweet old thing like Doris, who played all day with her collection of ribbons and feathers and plastic hairclips. Beth was angry.

Kate was angry, too. 'What was Mum thinking of, anyway?' she burst out. 'What a *stupid* thing to do, telling her troubles to some crackpot fortune teller. If she can't run the place and make it pay, then sell it, for God's sake, and buy something smaller. Stop struggling, just live like an ordinary person.'

'She says no one would buy it,' said Mick. 'It's too big for a family house, but not posh enough to attract a business buyer.'

'How does she know? She hasn't even tried, she just makes excuses. The place could be a nursing home or something. And don't give me that stuff about her keeping it going because it was her and Dad in it together – I'm fed up with the brave little woman act. And anyway,' she added, 'that's a goner now the wonderful Donald is on the scene.' She brooded for a few minutes as they walked, then said, 'I might as well tell you, Mick – I'm going to move in with Jake.'

'You mean, all the time?'

'Yes, all the time.'

'Oh.'

Bleakness descended like a chill mist. Not that

Kate had been around much lately, but now she wouldn't be coming home at all. Mick would be alone with Cathie and Donald and the dull Sheena, feeling like a stranger in a family that wasn't his.

'Don't look so gloomy,' said Kate. 'I'll see you at the Centre. And Jake's flat's only ten minutes away. It's in Fisher Street, off the shore road.'

Mick nodded, slightly cheered. A bolt-hole could be a good thing.

'Donald does my head in,' said Kate. 'He gave me a whole lecture about how I'd made a bum decision, not going to college, went on about qualifications and security. Such a cheek. He's not my father. I said I'd go to uni when I was good and ready, and when I did I wouldn't be studying Hotel Management. He said what *would* I study then, and I said Chinese. That shut him up.'

'*Will* you study Chinese?' asked Mick, quite prepared to believe it. Kate might do anything.

'Don't be daft,' said Kate. Then she added, 'I don't know what I want to do. It won't be for a while, anyway, but I'd quite like to work with people like the ones at the Centre. Not just doling out tuna rolls. I'd like to understand about them. Do something to help.'

'Yes,' said Mick. A seagull landed on the railings by the sea and shuffled its feathers into place. There must be thousands of feathers on one bird, and just a single one would keep Doris happy for hours, turning it over and over in her fingers. 'I see what you mean,' he said.

Kate stayed for supper, even though Donald and Sheena were there. Halfway through the meal, she made her announcement about leaving home.

Cathie sighed. 'Well, I could see that was on the cards,' she said.

On the cards. Mick flinched inwardly at the phrase, but Cathie didn't seem aware of what she'd said.

'You've hardly been here for weeks except to get your washing done,' she went on. 'But I think you're making a mistake.'

'So what's new,' said Kate.

Donald looked up from his pork chop and said, 'As long as you're careful, Kate. Don't do anything daft, will you.'

Kate met his gaze boldly. 'Jake hasn't got AIDS, if that's what you mean,' she said. 'They did a blood test when he was in hospital. And I'm on the pill.'

Donald's ears turned red. 'I didn't mean—'

'Yes, you did,' said Kate. 'That's what people always mean.'

'What's the pill?' asked Sheena.

Donald's blush spread across his face, but Cathie said, 'It's to stop ladies from having babies if they don't want them.'

'I'd like a baby,' said Sheena. 'I'm going to have lots.' She pushed her plate away and Donald said, 'What's the matter with that pork chop?'

'Don't want it. Can I have some crisps?'

'No,' said Cathie.

'Jake's coming round with the van tomorrow to move my stuff,' said Kate, 'when I come back from work.'

'I could have done that for you,' said Donald.

Kate ignored him. 'Can I have the bedside light from my room? Jake hasn't got one.'

'I suppose so,' said Cathie.

'Thanks,' said Kate, and went on eating.

Mick looked at her and wished there was something he could say. It would have been so different if he'd been the one who was going. For him, Cathie would have been rushing round, suggesting things he could take, cutting sandwiches, insisting he must come home for weekends. It had always been like that. *Kate's so independent*, Cathie would tell people. *Even as a baby, she never liked being cuddled. Mickey was so different.*

Mick looked at his sister and saw how unconcerned she was looking, determined not to show any hurt. And Cathie's face wore exactly the same expression.

The next evening, Jake came round in the van belonging to the band. It was yellow, with CLUB CLASS painted on its sides in big black letters.

Mick helped take things out, mostly in plastic carriers, though there were some cardboard boxes as well. Donald wasn't around for once, and Mick wondered if he was offended. *Well, tough*, he thought.

When everything was in and Jake shut the van's doors, Cathie suddenly turned to Kate and hugged her. Micky heard her say, 'You can always come back, Kate. I mean – this is your home. You don't have to go.'

'I know,' Kate said. 'Don't be upset, Mum. It's not as if I'm far away.'

Jake, sitting in the van, looked through its open window at Mick and said, 'You want to come and help unload?'

'Sure,' said Mick. It would be better to go off with Kate and Jake than stand here and wave the van goodbye. Kate got in, and he climbed in beside her and shut the door. 'Won't be long, Mum,' he said.

Cathie's hands were gripped tightly together. 'Oh, do be careful,' she blurted out. Nobody laughed.

'Trust me,' Jake said easily. 'I used to be an ambulance driver.'

'Oh. Well – good.' Cathie stood back and waved as the van pulled out of the drive.

'Were you really an ambulance driver?' asked Mick.

'No,' said Jake. 'Sounds good, though, doesn't it? Rather an inspiration, I thought.'

Kate kissed him behind his ear and said, 'You're dreadful.'

'No, I'm not. She's gone in feeling better, hasn't she.'

'You're still a wicked liar,' Kate said contentedly.

'Lying isn't wicked,' said Jake. 'Who's to say there's only one truth, anyway? It's a silly idea. You're in charge of what you say, you can choose. I could have told your mum I've got eight penalty points and the van's tyres are bald, and she'd have freaked out.'

Mick felt a touch of panic. 'Is *that* true?'

'No,' Jake said again. 'But there you go, you

see. I can scare you if I want. I used to do it a lot, but I don't any more. Let people feel happy, why not?'

'They won't be happy if they find out they've been lied to,' said Kate.

Jake slowed at the junction with Union Street and looked both ways. 'That's up to them,' he said. 'They can believe what they like.' He drove across the road and started along the shore road on the other side.

Mick was trying to get his head round all this. It sounded impossibly simple. *You can believe what you like.* But how did you get rid of something you didn't want to believe?

Jake turned right again and stopped outside a block of flats that had patches of weeds under the windows.

'This is it,' said Kate.

Mick got out and went round to the back of the van, where Jake was opening the doors. He hauled out a cardboard box that had Kate's old teddy looking out of the top of it, and carried it across the pavement.

The flat was on the ground floor. It was darkish inside because the curtains were drawn, but when Jake switched on the light, Mick saw that the walls were hung with Indian bedspreads. On all four sides of him, there were patterns of flowers and gods and elephants, black, purple, deep blue, red and brown.

'Saves a lot of bother,' Jake said as Mick stared round. 'When I move, I just take the decor with me.'

'There's horrible wallpaper underneath,' Kate explained. 'And the people who lived here before had kids who'd scribbled on it with felt-tip. You'd never paint over it, that stuff comes through everything.'

There was a faint smell of something between joss-sticks and scorched carpet, and Mick thought it was probably pot. Danny's big brother smoked it. Mick didn't much fancy smoking anything. He'd tried a cigarette once but it made him cough and he couldn't see that it was worth spending hard-earned money on. He went back out to the van.

It didn't take long to bring all Kate's things in. Jake dumped the last two carrier bags on the sofa and said, 'So there you are. Moved in.'

'Yes,' said Kate.

She and Jake stood and looked at each other, then Jake said, 'I never thought you'd do it, you know. You're a brave girl, taking up with a cretin like me.'

Kate just smiled, then she put her arms round Jake's neck and kissed him.

Mick thought he'd better be going.

'Stop for a coffee?' Kate suggested as he moved to the door. 'Or a Coke or something?'

He shook his head. It was obvious they wanted to be on their own. 'Another time,' he said.

'Well, thanks for helping, anyway,' said Kate.

'Run you home if you like,' Jake offered.

'Don't worry – it's no distance.'

Kate opened the front door for him. 'You can come round any time,' she said. 'You're always welcome, you know that. If things get a bit tacky at home, just turn up, OK?'

'OK,' said Mick.

'You've got the phone number?'

'Yes, you gave it to me before.'

There wasn't anything else to say.

'See you, then,' said Kate.

'Sure.'

Mick crossed the road then looked back to wave, but the door was already shut.

Nine

Walking back across the green, Mick mentally kicked himself. Why hadn't he stayed for a cup of coffee? Kate and Jake had all the time in the world to be on their own together, another ten minutes wouldn't have mattered. When he was a kid, Cathie had always told him it was good to be unselfish, but in fact nobody ever noticed and you ended up feeling a prat. He sat down on a bench, staring out to sea with his hands pushed into his jacket pockets. No need to go home right away. Donald would probably have turned up by now, so Cathie would be all right.

She doesn't need me any more.

The thought struck him so hard that it felt like a thump in the stomach. Cathie had someone else to share her concerns with. She hadn't complained to Mick about anything for weeks. Not since that day when the power failed and Donald came on the scene.

Mick knew he should be glad. Right now, he was sitting here almost in the hope that the electrician's van would arrive and Donald would do the listening. But where did that leave Mick? He had no purpose now, he just watched from outside while his mother put her arm round Sheena, a girl who loved to be cuddled, or reached up to take a fleck of plaster from Donald's rather sparse hair.

A worse idea washed into Mick's mind like one wave of the sea following another. *She'd be better off without me.* The only thing that stopped Cathie from relaxing happily into her new family was the fear that they were connected with the fate hanging over Mick. He got up uneasily and walked across to the rusted ornamental railing at the edge of the green, then leaned his folded arms on it. If Cathie had to choose between him and Donald, she'd go for Mick every time – or would she? On that first afternoon when he'd nearly caught them holding hands, she'd been so frantic about the idea that Donald was part of the prediction, she'd offered to send him away – but she hadn't. Right enough, it had been Mick who pointed out that it wouldn't make any difference, but the very next day, he'd come home from school to find Donald and Sheena sitting at the table. It would probably have been the same whatever he'd said. Maybe that was Cathie's destiny.

Not that he could blame her. She'd had years of being on her own, it was reasonable enough to want to be happy. The thing that spoiled it was Mick and this crazy business that hung round him. As Kate had said, *We won't shake it off until we've dealt with what's causing it.*

That's what I've got to do, Mick thought. *Get to grips with it somehow. Make it either happen or go away.* He needed to test what the fortune teller had said. If she was right, then the sooner it happened, the better. He would be out of the way, and Cathie could get on with her new life, once she'd got over her grieving. But if the woman called Verity Rose was wrong, it was high time to sweep the whole thing away and forget it.

There was only one person he could ask – old Beth.

The cafeteria at the Centre was in the big room used by a playgroup in the mornings, so it always smelt a bit of nappies and spilt yoghurt or whatever it was that people spooned into their toddlers. But it was lunchtime now. The toys had been stacked in the Wendy House and Kate with a couple of helpers had put up the card tables, each with a checked blue cloth and a plastic menu card, though what was on offer never changed except for the daily soup, and that was written on the blackboard.

Mick knew this was going to be difficult. He collected a ham and cheese toastie from Kate at the counter and told her what he was going to do.

'Best of luck,' she said. 'I'll try to find Duncan – you'll probably need him.'

'Why?'

'He speaks Gaelic.'

Old Beth was sitting at a table in the far corner, with Muggins on her lap as usual. Mick approached nervously. 'Is it all right if I sit here?' He almost hoped she'd say no – but she didn't, just took a piece of tuna from the roll she was eating and gave it to the cat.

Mick sat down. He took a bite of his toastie and wondered what to say. Old Beth glanced at him out of her pale, almost colourless eyes then went on chomping untidily at her tuna roll. A lot of her teeth were missing.

Minutes went by. Mick had finished his toastie before he managed to get any words together. He stood, up, holding his empty plate, and cleared his throat uneasily. 'Cup of tea?'

Old Beth looked at him and frowned.

'*Tea*,' Mick repeated, miming the picking up of a cup. 'Would you like a cup of tea?'

'Aye.'

That was something, anyway.

'Any luck?' Kate asked him when he went back to the counter.

'I haven't started yet. Can't seem to get going.'

'You'll have to speak slowly. Just ask her if the cards are always right, or if there could have been a mistake. D'you want a Coke?'

'Please. And a tea for Beth.'

He carried the drinks back to the table. Beth put two spoonfuls of sugar in her tea, stirred and sipped then nodded. 'Thank you,' she said.

It was a start.

'I wanted to ask you something,' said Mick. 'It's about fortune telling.'

Beth frowned.

'Cards,' said Mick. He mimed dealing from a pack. 'Tarot.'

'No cards here.' Her voice was deep and husky.

'I know. I don't want you to tell my fortune, it's just a question.'

He'd spoken too fast. Beth sipped her tea, watching him, but said nothing. Mick had another go.

'My mother – *mother*, OK? Went to a fortune

teller. Cards.' He mimed again. 'But are they always right? Could she have made a mistake?'

Old Beth stroked Muggins and tickled him under his chin, and Mick sat back in despair. This was getting him nowhere.

From behind him, a voice said, 'Can I help?'

Duncan was standing there, round-shouldered and scrawny in some ancient jacket that might once have been black. He had a newspaper tucked under his arm and wore glasses with such thick lenses that hardly any gaze seemed to come through them. He pulled out a chair and sat down.

'*Ciamar a tha thu an diugh, Beth?*'

'*Tha mi gu math.*'

Mick didn't understand a word of the Gaelic that ran in a soft ripple between them, but he saw how Beth's face lost its vagueness.

Duncan turned his face to Mick. 'Your sister told me about your difficulty. Shall I ask Beth for you?'

'Please,' said Mick. Duncan was the ugliest man he had ever seen. His grooved, sagging face looked grey under its thick growth of stubble, and his lower lip drooped heavily, revealing its red inner lining – but Mick saw what Kate had meant when she said Duncan was clever. The questions he put to old Beth were fluent and careful, and he nodded as she replied, storing the information.

'She says the cards never lie,' he told Mick when Beth came to a stop. 'But people don't always understand them.'

Never lie. Mick swallowed hard.

'It's a question of how they are interpreted,' Duncan went on. 'A wise teller will see more than a stupid one. You need insight, she says. And experience.'

'But – the woman my mother went to see – could she have been wrong?'

Duncan put the question to old Beth, who shrugged. Mick knew the reply even before it was translated.

'She didn't see the cards, so she can't know.'

Beth was talking again, faster now and looking quite angry. Duncan listened then explained. 'She's very cross with whoever it was for being so unprofessional. A fortune teller should never break bad news like that. If a death is in the cards, they should just say, "There will be a death". The cards will never tell whose death it is, and it's not for the teller to guess.'

'But *will* there be a death?' Mick demanded. If old Beth really had the Sight, she herself might know.

She understood his question without Duncan's interpretation, and looked away, frowning and stroking the cat. She muttered a reply, but Duncan had to lean close to catch it. When he sat back, he, too, was frowning.

'There is a death to come,' he said. 'But she thinks it may not be yours.' And he added, 'You mustn't worry.'

Muggins suddenly leapt off Beth's lap, causing instant chaos. Beth heaved herself to her feet with a great floundering of shawls and cardigans, not bothering to push her chair back. It fell over and the table lurched, and a trailing woolly fringe knocked her empty cup over, spilling its dregs. Mick grabbed for the milk jug as Beth's shawl swept past it, but Beth herself didn't give the table a glance. She went after the cat, chirruping and clicking her fingers.

Duncan's thick glasses were looking at Mick in what seemed to be concern. 'There are deaths all the time,' he pointed out. 'Every day, people die, and others are born. You mustn't be afraid.'

'No,' Mick agreed. He tried to smile. 'It's OK. I'm kind of – used to it.'

The bottle-bottom lenses went on regarding him for a few moments, then Duncan got up, tucked his paper under his arm and walked away.

* * *

The upstairs bathroom, which was also a toilet, was in a particularly bad state, with all the paintwork pitted and flaking. There were already tiles round the bath, very old ones, veined with grey lines, and the rest of the walls were panelled with ancient tongue-and-groove planking, painted a dozen times over the years. Gavin thought it would look great if the tongue-and-groove was stripped down and varnished, so he'd given Mick a gas blowlamp and shown him how to use it. The trick was to get a patch hot enough so it was brown and bubbling before you tried to scrape it off. Anything less than properly boiling, and the layers underneath didn't shift.

Mick turned on the gas and lit the roaring flame, then picked up his triangular scraper. He had several of different shapes, but this one was the best because the points got into the narrow gaps between the planks. He started work. Scraps of what old Beth had said were sticking with paint-like obstinacy in his mind. *The cards never lie. There is a death to come.* If only the cat hadn't done a runner just at that moment, he might have learned something more useful. As it was, Beth had just added to the uncertainty of the whole thing, and to the dread that nagged at him all the time.

'Blast!'

A dollop of sizzling paint had fallen on the back of his hand. Mick shook it off quickly, but a scrap of it had stuck, burning its way into his skin. He put the blowlamp on the floor and turned to the dirty wash-basin, struggling to turn the tap on. It was stiff. He tried harder, and a jet of water shot out, splashing over his hand and down the front of his jeans and his T-shirt. He took a step back to avoid the spray, still grappling with the tap, trying this time to turn it down a bit.

The smell of scorching caught his attention before he felt the searing pain on the side of his leg, just above the ankle. He gasped and jumped sideways, then looked down and saw that the blowlamp had set the leg of his jeans on fire. He beat at it with an old towel then heaved his foot into the basin under the still-running tap. Smoke came up, and there was a small hiss as the water hit the smouldering fabric.

Careless of the water that flooded into his trainer, Mick put the plug in the basin and let it fill. He stood there on one leg for some time, sloshing water through the charred hole in his jeans, then lifted his dripping foot out and sat down on the edge of the bath. He leaned down and turned the blowlamp off, and inspected the damage. There was a livid weal across the side of his leg, already blistered and weeping, and it hurt so much that the small burn on the back of his hand was nothing at all.

Gavin came in and stopped in the doorway. 'Oh, my God,' he said. 'What have you done?'

'Bit of an accident,' said Mick.

He stayed in the Centre for the rest of the afternoon with his foot in a bowl of cold water in Gavin's office, being fed cups of tea and chocolate biscuits by Kate.

'Mum's going to do her nut,' she said.

'I know.' Gavin had said he should go to Casualty, but Mick drew the line at that. What if they took him home in an ambulance or phoned Cathie to say he was there? She'd go berserk. 'But it was my own fault,' Mick said. 'I was just careless.' Even as he spoke, he knew the argument didn't hold up. Accidents could be the working of fate – he'd said so himself when Kevin had his mishap with the chisel.

When it was time to go home, Gavin lathered Mick's leg with some sort of cream from the First Aid kit then broke open a sterile dressing and taped it on. Just for good measure, he bandaged the whole thing, then insisted on running Mick home in the car.

As bad luck had it, Cathie was setting tables in the dining room when Gavin drew up, and she saw Mick get out. She rushed to the front door and opened it, then stood aghast as Mick came up the drive. He'd managed to persuade Gavin not to come in.

Cathie saw the white bandage and ruined jeans at once, and her hands flew to her face.

'It's all right,' Mick said quickly. 'Don't panic. It's just a bit of a burn, that's all.'

'But what were you doing? How did you burn yourself?'

Mick led the way through to the kitchen, trying hard not to limp, and explained what had happened.

'Well, that's it,' said Cathie. 'You're not going back to that place. I'd never have a moment's peace.'

'Look, I could have burned myself right here in the kitchen,' Mick argued, 'but you wouldn't say I had to keep out of it for ever, would you?'

'I might,' said Cathie. Her eyes were bright with tears.

'Oh, Mum, don't cry.' Mick put his arms round her and felt how she was shaking. 'I'm all right. It didn't happen.'

She nodded convulsively, but she couldn't reply. He knew what she was thinking. *Not this time. But it will.*

Ten

The next morning, Cathie insisted on taking Mick to the doctor. They waited for a long time in a room full of mothers with snotty-nosed toddlers, then were called in. Dr McKinnon unwrapped the bandage and peeled off the dressing, which had stuck a bit.

'That's fine,' he said, though Mick thought the whole thing looked a mess. 'Nice and clean. I'll write you a prescription for sterile dressings and cream. If you pop out and see Nurse, she'll do your leg for you now.' He binned the old bandages and added, 'Take a couple of paracetemol if it's very sore. Tell the next one to come in, will you?'

'Thanks,' said Mick.

Cathie wouldn't hear of him going to the Centre, but Mick persuaded her that he could at least take Rusty out.

'Not far,' Cathie said. 'Just across the green, all right?'

'OK.' Mick didn't in fact want to go very far. He wondered why going to the doctor always made you feel more ill when you came out than you did when you went in.

He walked across the grass then down the steps to the beach. Rusty tore in and out of the shallow waves, barking madly as he always did, and Mick followed him along the sand to where a stream of water ran out from a tunnel under the road. That was as far as he could go without wading, so he turned up the further flight of steps, back on to the green – and came face to face with Chloë Johnson, sitting on a bench reading a magazine, with a baby in a buggy beside her.

'Hi,' said Mick. He nodded at the baby. 'That yours?'

'Do you mind?' Chloë said indignantly. 'I look after him for Maureen next door. She's got a job at the launderette. I haven't seen you around – you been away?'

Mick shook his head. He used to go and stay with Gran in Ayr during the holiday, but since she went doolally that had stopped. 'Have you?' he asked.

'We'd a week in Ibiza. It was great.'

'I've been working at the Drop In Centre,' Mick said. 'Only I burned my leg with a blowlamp yesterday, so I'm taking the day off.'

'Sounds nasty.' Chloë was still scanning her magazine. 'When's your birthday?'

'March the third. Why?'

'Tell you your horoscope. Mine's really boring. It says I shouldn't rush into any major financial decisions. Got to be joking.' She ran her finger down the columns, each headed with a sign of the zodiac. 'Here we are. You're a Pisces, right? The fish.'

'Dunno.' He'd never been interested in all that.

'It's the last sign of the year,' Chloë explained. 'You're supposed to be the wise ones because you've had time to learn from all the others.' She was scanning the print as she spoke, and at the end of it she raised her eyebrows and said, 'Ooh, funny.'

'Go on,' said Mick. 'Tell me the worst.'

'It's not exactly bad,' said Chloë. 'Just kind of strange. It says, "Don't let your vivid imagination distort the picture you receive from others – the task of all Piceans is to see clearly. A crisis awaits you at the end of this month, and you will need faith and strength." ' She looked up from the magazine. 'So what's this crisis, d'you reckon?'

Mick couldn't answer. *The picture you receive from others.* That must mean the cards. But was *he* distorting the picture? That seemed unfair. He hadn't even seen the horrible cards, so how could he distort what they said? But as to the coming crisis – that seemed all too probable.

'What's the matter?' asked Chloë. 'You look worried.'

'I'm OK.'

Chloë stared at him, frowning. 'There's something wrong, isn't there,' she said. 'Come on, you can tell me. I won't let on to anyone else, promise.'

'It's just – things have been a bit weird.' And then Mick found himself telling her all about it.

Chloë didn't interrupt, and she didn't laugh. When he got to the end she said, 'Wow. That's scary.'

Mick felt rather comforted. He'd kept telling himself there was nothing to be afraid of, so it was a relief that someone else found it frightening, too.

'If all that had happened to me and my mum, I'd be frantic,' said Chloë. 'What are you going to do?'

'I don't know,' Mick admitted. That was the worst of it. There was nothing to get hold of. No way to fight back.

Chloë shivered. 'It's so creepy, with this guy Donald and everything, just like she said. And then your accident.'

'It didn't get me, though. I'm still alive.' Mick was hanging on to this thought. The thing that threatened him hadn't made the most of its chance. Another few seconds, and he might not have been able to get his foot under the tap in time. The flames could have run up his leg and reached his paint-stained T-shirt and then – he shut his eyes against the vision of a fire-engulfed figure and of flames licking along the wooden walls, smoke billowing from the small window, fire filling the room, bursting out through the door, maybe setting light to the whole house. Nobody could have saved him.

Chloë glanced again at the horoscope. 'What do they mean, *imagination*? You didn't imagine any of this, it really happened.'

She had put her finger on the thing that was bothering Mick.

'I could be sort of joining in with what the fortune teller imagined,' he said. 'I mean, it could be just imagination that fate works at all. Look at that stuff in your magazine. Somebody writes it, don't they? So they've made it up.'

'Yes, but only after they've looked at where the

stars and planets are,' Chloë pointed out. 'They say we're all influenced by much bigger forces. All the same,' she added, 'what they say can't be right for everyone, can it? Look at me and my financial decisions. I don't have any finance. Right now, I've got forty-two pence.'

'You still have to decide what to spend it on, though,' said Mick. 'You can't expect the stars to know how much money you've got.'

'S'pose not.' Chloë pondered. Her thick fringe of hair came down to her eyebrows, a reddy-brown colour a bit like Rusty's coat. 'It's just a kind of game, really,' she said. 'I love it when they say something and it really fits. It's like, "Yes, that's me." As if there's something out there that knows all about you and wants to be helpful.'

'Or doesn't,' said Mick. 'What if it knows all about you and it's trying to do you in?'

'Horrible.' Chloë read the horoscope again, then looked up. 'You're going to be all right, though – you must be. It says you'll need faith and strength to deal with this crisis. That means you can fend it off.'

'But how?' Mick was starting to feel exasperated. 'What do they mean? What are you supposed to have faith in?'

'Could be God, I suppose,' said Chloë. 'People

pray for things like getting a bike for Christmas, don't they? He's supposed to be the one who's in charge of everything.'

'That means God's the same thing as fate.' This was getting worse. 'Anyway, it's not God who gives you a bike for Christmas, it's your parents.'

Chloë looked a bit shocked. 'Yes, but it could be God who makes it possible for them to earn the money,' she said. 'You can't be sure it isn't.'

You can't be sure. Every time Mick tried to think the whole thing through, that's what it came back to. You couldn't know. You could believe what you liked, and nobody could prove it was wrong. Or right, either.

'Anyway,' Chloë went on, 'we'll be back at school next week, and you'll be all right there. You can't have a crisis at school, it's too organised.'

'There was Kevin and his chisel. And there's things happen outside school – look at Debbie's little brother.'

'Oh, all *right*,' said Chloë, losing patience. 'You don't have to keep on thinking about it, you'll only make it seem worse. I mean, fortune tellers aren't qualified or anything. People don't pass exams in reading the crystal ball or whatever, it's not like doctors or teachers. You'll either have to forget it or else do something about it.'

'But *how* can I do something?'

'Go and see the fortune teller,' Chloë said as if it was obvious. 'Ask her if she's sure she got it right.'

Not again, thought Mick. Consulting old Beth had been bad enough, and it hadn't improved things at all. 'What if she says, yes, she's sure?'

'Then you're back where you were. It wouldn't be any worse. Where does she live?'

'In Union Street, next to the betting shop.'

'Come on.' Chloë pushed the magazine into the rack under the buggy and stood up. 'Let's go now. I'll come with you, I'd love to see her.'

Mick felt a wave of panic come over him. This was all happening too fast – but as he cast around frantically for an excuse, the baby made a spluttering noise then began to cry.

'Oh, rats,' said Chloë. 'It's coming up to his feed time, but I hoped he'd go a bit longer.' She jiggled the buggy and said 'Ssh,' but the baby went on bawling. Red fists came out from under the covers and shook angrily. Mick looked at it gratefully.

'I'll have to take him home,' said Chloë. 'Maureen comes back at lunchtime – she'll feed him.' She kicked the buggy's brake up with her toe. 'But you must go and see her, Mick. And tell me all about it, right?'

'Right,' said Mick. 'See you.'

He watched Chloë push the buggy away across the green. After a few minutes, she might have been anyone, just another girl with a baby. He thought what a lot of people there were, millions of them, all as alike as ants in the distance, and all of them at the centre of their own lives, not knowing what would happen next, but hoping it wouldn't be bad.

Rusty stood up and gave his wet coat a shake. He knew there would be a biscuit for him when they got in. 'All right,' said Mick, and started out for home.

Cathie was sitting at the kitchen table with Donald. She smiled at Mick when he came in and said, 'All right?'

'Fine.'

Donald looked up from his coffee. 'Don't ever put a blowlamp down without turning it off,' he said. 'It's one of the first things you learn.'

All right, Mick thought irritably. *I've learned, thanks.*

'Your mum and I were talking,' Donald went on. 'She's a bit worried about your future.' He

112

glanced at Cathie, who gave him a trusting look.

Mick wondered why he was sounding so important about it. If Cathie had confided in him about the fortune teller, so what? But it didn't seem to be about that at all.

'If you're going to college,' Donald was saying, 'you need to pick a course that's some use. There's plenty of people with degrees come out of uni and straight on to the dole queue. You need a trade. Something there's always a call for. See, you're practical, Mick – never mind the blowlamp, we all do daft things sometimes. So I said to your mum, if you'd like to work part-time with me, weekends and the odd evening while you're still at school, I could start you off. Teach you some of the basics, pay you a bit of pocket money. Not a lot to start with, but I'd put it up when you got more useful. Then when you leave school, if you study electrics properly you could keep on with me in your spare time. Better than a student loan that puts you in debt for years. But it's up to you. No pressure – but think it over, right?'

'Right,' said Mick. He ought to jump at the offer. It was the nearest thing to a real job he was likely to get. He'd never thought he'd be an electrician, though. It wasn't like being a vet – but that might have been just a dream, anyway.

'It would have to be unofficial,' Donald said. 'I can't afford to take on a registered apprentice. You've to have a proper workshop for that, with toilets and all that stuff. Paperwork, insurance. A small business like mine, it's too much. You see what I mean?'

'Yes,' said Mick. The burn on his leg was throbbing, and something at the back of his mind was grinning in an evil sort of way. *You think you can plan ahead? You may not even be here.* 'I'll have to think about it,' he said. 'But thanks, anyway.'

'I think it's a really generous offer,' said Cathie.

'Yes,' Mick agreed. 'Yes, it is.' And then he escaped upstairs.

So Cathie didn't mind the idea of him poking screwdrivers into live sockets or falling off ladders, he thought as he stared out of his bedroom window. She thought no harm could come to him in Donald's care. Or else she was sick of the whole business – though that didn't seem likely when she had been so upset over the blowlamp affair. *I'm the one who's sick of it*, Mick thought. He was sick of questions that couldn't be answered, sick of being afraid and of telling himself there was nothing to be afraid of. *If it's going to happen, let's get it over with.* Chloë was right, he must go

114

and see the fortune teller. Right now, while his determination lasted.

He swung away from the window and went out of his room and quietly down the first flight of stairs, then leaned over the banister and listened. Cathie and Donald were still talking in the kitchen. He went down the next flight, the one the visitors used that led to the hall, and let himself out of the front door, closing it behind him as silently as he could. Then he walked past Donald's van in the drive and set off for Union Street.

Eleven

A race commentary was being shouted excitedly from the TV set in the betting shop, and Mick had to put his ear close to the perforated grille of the entry-phone before he could hear the crackling voice that answered his ring.

'Who is it?'

'My name's Michael Finn. My mother—'

'Who?'

'You saw my mother. You told her fortune.'

'If you want a reading, you can make an appointment.'

'I don't want a reading. I want to see you.'

'I don't see people out of hours.'

'BUT YOU SAID I WAS GOING TO DIE!' Mick yelled. A man in the betting shop turned his head from the screen to give him an odd look, and the door buzzed and opened an inch.

Mick went in and found himself confronted by a flight of shabbily-carpeted stairs. The door clicked shut behind him, taking most of the light with it. He started up towards the small landing above him.

The door on his right was opened by a woman with frizzy orange hair and blue-framed spectacles with fancy sides. Behind them, her eyes were jet black, as Cathie had said. 'I'm having my lunch,' she said.

It was barely twelve, early for lunch, Mick thought. He said, 'I'm sorry. I just need to ask you something.'

She stared at him for a moment then said, 'You'd better come in.'

He followed her into a small living room, and recognised Cathie's description of it – brown and yellow carpet, three-piece suite, lava lamp thing on the mantelpiece, only it was switched off so the bubbles weren't moving. There was an open newspaper on the table by the window and a plate with cold meat and a half-finished tomato, together with a packet of crispbread and a bottle of salad cream.

'What do you want to know?' the woman asked. She wore a loudly-patterned silk shirt over black trousers, and she was quite old, Mick realised. Her mouth was wrinkled under the bright lipstick, and the roots of the orange hair were grey.

'It's just . . . you told my mother's fortune. And you said—'

'What was her name?'

'Cathie Finn.'

'What does she look like?'

'She's got dark hair with silver streaks in it. She wears jeans mostly.' Mick struggled to find something that would trigger the woman's memory. 'She came at lunchtime, same as me. Or just after.'

'Ah, yes.' It seemed to have worked. 'Runs a hotel on her own? Dead husband?'

'Yes.' Mick found himself hating the woman. She couldn't be called Verity Rose, he thought. It sounded much too sweet.

'Most extraordinary cards,' the fortune teller said. 'I've never had such a clear message.'

Mick stared at her in dread. This was not what he had hoped to hear. He cleared his throat nervously. 'I just wondered . . .' he said, but couldn't find the words to go on.

'Wondered what?'

'If it was right, what you said. About me dying and everything.'

'Oh, yes,' the woman said emphatically. 'It was so strong, there was hardly any interpretation needed. Quite extraordinary. Your mother sensed

118

it of course, she's quite receptive.'

'But – are you sure?'

'I've never been more certain.' Verity Rose adjusted her glasses with both hands. Her fingernails were painted scarlet. 'The cards showed a classic blocked situation. Something had to go before her life could start to flow again, you see what I mean, dear? A sacrifice had to be made. When the final cards came up, I hardly had to tell her what they said. She knew at once. "It's my son, isn't it," she said.'

Mick couldn't believe he was being told all this so calmly, as if it was a matter of mere interest.

'And she was right, of course,' the woman went on. 'A sacrifice has to be the thing that is closest.'

Mick felt paralysed. Nobody else could take that place. Not Kate or Jake or Rusty. Probably not even Donald. 'It's got to be me,' he said.

The fortune teller looked at him, still quite detached. 'You mustn't worry about it,' she said. 'You have lived many times before, and you will live again. By the way,' she added, 'has the man arrived yet? He was very clear in the cards.'

'Yes,' said Mick, dry-mouthed. 'His name's Donald.'

She nodded. 'The rest should follow quite soon, then.'

Quite soon. The words settled in his stomach like a lead weight.

'You must welcome this new experience,' Verity Rose said. Her black eyes glittered with a kind of excitement behind the fancy glasses.

She's mad, Mick thought. *Totally bonkers.* But it didn't help.

'Now, dear, if you don't mind . . .' She dusted an imaginary crumb from the front of her shirt, reminding him that her lunch had been interrupted.

Mick turned to the door. She opened it for him and said, 'I'll make this free of charge, but it's normally five pounds for a reading. And I don't do follow-ons.'

His feet didn't seem to belong to him, but somehow he was out on the landing. 'Thanks,' he managed to say.

'Look forward with joy to what is coming,' the fortune teller said, and smiled at him. There was lipstick on her teeth. Then she shut the door.

Each footstep seemed to cause a jolt of dull pain in Mick's head, and the sky's dazzle was behind his eyes and in his brain, breaking his thoughts into jagged fragments. *The rest should follow quite soon.*

A container lorry drove past on its way to the harbour, and the dusty wind that followed it pulled at him as if it wanted to suck him into its wake. Mick could see himself spinning like a scrap of rubbish in the street, blown about until he fetched up on the barbed wire behind the transport depot where grey rags of plastic hung and fluttered in the sea wind.

At the bottom of Union Street he hesitated. Cathie would panic if she discovered he'd gone out. Then he almost laughed. *Too late for panic now.* In some weird way, he seemed to be watching himself from outside, taking an interest as detached as the fortune teller's in a boy called Michael Finn. And the boy himself was watching the moments of his life as they ran past. He was trying to slow them down and notice each one, because he knew that before long, they would stop.

Mick crossed the road and headed away past the back of the warehouses, out along the shore road where long grass grew among the sand, making for the flat in Fisher Street. He wanted to talk to Kate. Then he remembered she'd be at the Centre, further on down the road, and paused. They wouldn't be expecting to see him – Cathie had phoned to say he wasn't coming in. *What the hell*, he thought. He could always say he was feeling better, or feeling bored or something. He walked on, past the junction with Fisher Street – then stopped again.

The faint sound of a jazz saxophone floated through the quiet afternoon. Mick listened, fascinated. It must be Jake – he'd never heard him play before. He turned up Fisher Street and moved closer, as helplessly as a hooked fish towed by a line. The tumbling notes sounded effortless, but sometimes a phrase would be repeated several times, in search of some small change that Mick couldn't detect. He was across the road from the flat now, and the music filled his mind so that there was no room for anything else.

The playing stopped, and Jake was at the window, holding the sax on its strap round his neck. He saw Mick, with no sign of surprise, and raised a hand in greeting then tilted an imaginary cup. *Come in for a coffee*? Mick found himself walking across the road towards the door.

'Hi,' Jake said. 'How's the leg? Kate told me about your accident.'

'It's OK.' Mick followed him into the tiny kitchen and watched while Jake switched the kettle on and rinsed a couple of mugs from among the unwashed ones that occupied the sink. He wasn't sure that he should have come in. He didn't know Jake very well. The lean face and straggling hair made him look very different from most people, and Mick had the feeling that he wouldn't want to bother with anyone who bored him. Mick had wanted to see Kate, not Jake. *Look forward with joy to what is coming.* He found he was feeling rather shaky. With an effort, he managed to say, 'I heard you playing. It sounded great.'

'You have to keep practising or your lip goes. Milk and sugar?' He'd made coffee, not asking what Mick would like, but it didn't matter.

'Yes, please.'

'Kate's at the Centre.'

'I know. I didn't mean to come in, really.'

'Well, that's cool.' Jake went back into the other room with Mick behind him. 'Clear a space,' he said vaguely. 'Take the weight off your feet.'

Mick shifted a sweatshirt and some CDs off an armchair and sat down.

'Thanks for that record, by the way,' Jake said. 'Billie Holiday. What a woman. One of the great hurtables.'

'Hurtables?'

'Some people sing like they've got all the answers,' said Jake. 'Great, of course, but kind of tough. Tony Bennett, Sinatra – the classic oldies,

123

doing it their way. Brilliant technique, well in charge of it all. But the ones like Billie Holiday know what being alive is all about. You never get on top of it, not really. All you can do is enjoy the sweet moments and keep your head down.'

There was a long pause. With the small part of his mind that wasn't flying around in panic, Mick found himself wishing he'd got into music properly. All those school keyboards with the letters of the scale written on them were a turn-off, somehow. 'I wish I could play,' he said.

'Teach you if you like,' Jake said casually.

Mick shook his head, half smiling. Too late for that sort of thing. He might not even be here.

'No, honest,' said Jake. 'If you really want to. It's the wanting that matters, you see, otherwise you'd never get through the slog of learning. Even when you're reasonably good at it, you still hear music in your head that's just out of reach. Still wanting.'

A faint excitement stirred. 'Do you think I could?'

'No problem. You need to start on the clarinet. Same fingering except the sax overblows for the upper register.'

Mick had no idea what he was talking about.

Jake got up and started shifting some of the

piled stuff in the room. 'I've got a clarinet here somewhere,' he said. 'Haven't played it for years – you can borrow it and welcome.' He gave up and sat down again. 'Kate'll find it. She knows where all my stuff is, she's amazing.'

'Yes,' said Mick. His sister really was rather amazing if she could make any sense of this chaotic man. It occurred to him that the fortune teller had never mentioned Kate. Perhaps Cathie hadn't mentioned her, either. *'It's my son, isn't it,'* she'd said. *A sacrifice has to be the thing that is closest*. He shut his eyes as a fresh wave of dread came over him.

Jake had picked up his sax again, but he asked, 'D'you want some lunch or something?'

'No, thanks. I'd better get back, I didn't tell Mum I was coming out.'

'She's a bit excitable, your mum,' said Jake.

'Is she?' Mick would never have thought of that word.

'Nice lady, though.' Jake played a ripple of notes then added, 'Stick around if you like. I don't mind.'

'Better not. Thanks for the coffee.'

'Welcome.' Jake started playing again.

Mick took the two mugs out to the kitchen and washed them. He looked at the other plates and cups and wondered if he should do those as well. Kate was probably fed up with kitchen work by the time she came home from the Centre. But thoughts of Cathie nagged at him, so he dried his hands on a grubbyish towel and let himself out of the front door. The easy-sounding jazz followed him back along the street in the sunshine.

Twelve

Mick went back to the Centre the next day and got on with the bathroom. He was extremely careful with the blowlamp.

In the cafeteria at lunchtime he became uneasily aware that old Beth was watching him. She sat as huddled and still as ever with the cat on her lap and an empty teacup in front of her, but her eyes were fixed on Mick. She didn't look away if he met her gaze, just went on surveying him as if he was a TV set with an interesting programme. Only Mick didn't know what she was seeing.

It was the same at the tea break. Mick went and found Duncan and asked him if he could find out what Beth was up to.

Half an hour later, Duncan appeared at the bathroom door, looking even more crumpled and droopy than usual. Mick turned the blowlamp off and waited.

The ugly man seemed to be having difficulty

in finding words. He produced an immensely dirty handkerchief and wiped his nose with it then took his time over stuffing it back into his pocket. Then he said, 'I wouldn't take too much notice.'

'Course not,' Mick said bravely, but his heart sank.

'She speaks of a death,' Duncan said, and there was a hint of old Beth's Gaelic rhythm in his words. 'She says it is coming very close.'

It was just what Mick had expected. He was almost beyond fear now, just deeply and painfully unhappy. 'It's me, isn't it,' he said. 'The one who's going to die.'

'She didn't say that. Only that it's coming close.' Duncan was precise, and Mick thought about the word more carefully.

'Like, close to where we are or close, coming soon?' Not that it mattered.

Duncan considered the question carefully. 'Beth's Gaelic is a little different from mine,' he said. 'She is from North Uist. But I think it could mean either. Close. Near. Not far away.'

Not far away. Mick sat down on the edge of the bath. His joints felt oddly weak.

Duncan didn't register any expression. His sagging mouth was never able to smile and the deep grooves of his face didn't change, but the eyes behind the thick spectacles seemed to focus on Mick with more concern. 'You mustn't take it personally,' he said.

Mick almost laughed. How else was he to take it?

'You're not the dying sort,' Duncan said suddenly. 'It won't be you.' He seemed embarrassed by this little outburst and fumbled for his handkerchief again, dropping the newspaper he was carrying. He stooped for it clumsily but Mick got there first, afraid the man would crack his head on the wash-basin. He brushed off a few paint-peelings and handed the paper back to Duncan, who tucked it under his arm again.

'Thanks for asking old Beth,' Mick said, 'and everything.' It had been nice of him to make that effort to sound encouraging.

Duncan hovered uncertainly as if about to say something else, then he turned and went out. Mick heard his uncertain footsteps finding their way down the stairs. He sat down on the bath's edge again. *You're not the dying sort.* But somewhere at the back of his mind, The Hanged Man swung calmly upside down, smiling at the sky.

He worked on for a bit, then decided it was

knocking-off time. He went down to the kitchen and found Kate, who was taking off her apron.

'Hi,' she said. 'How's your leg?'

'Getting better.' A burned leg was the least of his worries.

They went down the steps and out into the sunshine. Gulls wheeled in the blue sky and the water rippled brightly between the small boats in the harbour behind the old shipping office.

'Such an amazing summer,' Kate said. 'It seems like it'll go on for ever.'

Nothing goes on for ever, Mick thought. And the shakiness was back, because he loved it all so much, even the crisp bags and empty cans littering the sand between the long, pale grass. Every minute of it was to be treasured, but the minutes were ebbing away.

'So how have you been?' Kate asked. 'Anything new happened?'

'I went to see the fortune teller.' He hadn't been able to tell Jake, but he told Kate all about it, and about old Beth as well, and what Duncan had said.

They came to the junction with Fisher Street and stopped. Kate turned to face him and said, 'Quite honestly, Mick, I'm fed up with all this doom-mongering. What's the point? It's only making you unhappy, and it's all about nothing. I've no patience with it.'

'No,' said Mick. He felt very hurt. 'Sorry.'

'Don't be like that,' said Kate. 'It's just – well, there are more things to think about.' She frowned, then made up her mind. 'I may as well tell you. I'm going to have a baby.'

'Go on!' Mick was startled out of his own concerns. 'Hey, that's brilliant!'

Kate smiled, seeming relieved. 'Oh, good. I'm glad you're pleased. So am I. And Jake's over the moon.'

'I bet.' Then Mick thought of something. 'But didn't you say—'

'I was on the pill? Yes, I did. And I was, only I forgot a couple of times. I wasn't going to tell horrible Donald, though. It's none of his business. Mum doesn't know yet, either, so don't let on.'

'I won't,' Mick promised. 'I'll be an uncle! That's amazing.' *If I'm here.* But the thought was swamped in a rush of new terror for the little creature that waited to be born. Some babies died in their cots for no reason. Some never lived properly at all, dying even before they emerged into the world. *Don't you dare*, he said silently to the fate that waited somewhere in the blue sky. *It's me you're dealing with, not the baby.*

'It'll be born at the end of February,' Kate said. 'Somewhere near your birthday.' Then she went on, 'The only thing is, Jake feels bad about it interrupting my education. But I don't see that it matters which way round you do things. I can go to college later. I'll be more sure what I want to do then. You coming in for a cuppa?'

Mick shook his head. 'Better not. Mum was in a tizz when I got back from being at yours yesterday. I didn't tell her I was going out.' And he hadn't told her about going to see Verity Rose.

'You'll have to take a firm line,' said Kate. 'Things can't go on like this, Mick, it's ridiculous.'

'I know,' said Mick. *But what do I do about it?*

'See you tomorrow.' Kate touched his sleeve lightly and added, 'Take care.'

'I will. You, too.' He looked at her in sudden concern. 'Shouldn't you be – well, resting and stuff? Taking it easy?'

Kate laughed. 'Oh, Mick! You're such an old worrier. I'm fine. Stand by for a phone call tonight. Now I've told you I feel a bit better about telling Mum. She's not going to be pleased, though.'

Mick held up crossed fingers and she laughed again then walked away, turning to give him a wave.

* * *

They were watching a video when the phone rang, Mick in an armchair and Donald and Cathie on the sofa with Sheena cuddled between them. Cathie hit the pause button and picked up the phone. 'The Laurels Guest House – oh, hallo, Kate.'

Mick stared at the jiggling lines on the screen and wished he was somewhere else.

'You're what? Oh, you silly girl!' Cathie raised anguished eyebrows at Donald. 'How far on are you? . . . Well, that's not too bad, there's time to do something about it, but for goodness' sake don't wait too–' She broke off, listening in consternation. 'Kate, don't be ridiculous. You've no security, you're throwing away all your chances. And how do you think I feel, after all this struggle to bring you up decently? I'm not going to give everything up to look after your illegitimate– . . . what do you mean, you wouldn't ask? There's no need to be insulting.'

Mick got up and left the room, hoping they'd think he was going to the toilet. Donald glanced up at him, unsmiling, his round face creased with worry, but Cathie was too busy talking to notice.

Upstairs, he sat on his bed and listened to the sound of outraged conversation in the room

133

below. After a while, Cathie called him.

'Mickey? Come down here, please.'

In the sitting room the video was running again, but only Sheena was watching it, and even she had half an eye on the grown-ups.

'Do you know what Kate's just told me?' Cathie demanded.

'About the baby?' Mick tried to sound unconcerned. 'Yes, she said this afternoon.'

'And you kept it to yourself?' Cathie ran her fingers through her hair. 'I just don't understand what's going on.'

'Your sister wasn't very truthful, I'm afraid,' said Donald. 'She said she was taking precautions.'

'That wretched Jake,' said Cathie. 'I could wring his neck. And I'm sure he's a drug addict. You can always tell. These oh-so-relaxed people, they're all the same. Smoking pot and stuff. I don't want you going round there, Mick, I told you yesterday.'

Donald said, 'Don't get upset.'

'I'm not upset. It's just I don't want Mick getting into some terrible habit. It's so dangerous.'

To Mick's surprise, Donald said, 'It's fair enough for him to want to see his sister, Cathie.'

She looked at him and her shoulders drooped. 'I just want to keep him safe.'

'I know you do.' He put his hand over hers,

134

careless of Mick and Sheena watching. 'And I know why. It's been a bad time for you, an awful fear. But you have to put it behind you. Things happen or don't happen, that's all. There's no reason to it, no plan. You just have to take the days as they come.'

Cathie sighed. Then she leaned her head back and smiled at Donald. 'You're so sensible,' she said. 'What would I do without you?'

Mick got to his feet. 'I'll take the dog out,' he said.

He followed Rusty across the green. The evening light was fading, and for the first time in weeks, a line of heavy cloud was building up behind the dark shape of Broray. Mick toyed with the idea of walking out to the sea wall, but the burn on his leg was still sore – and Rusty had already disappeared down the steps to the beach. Mick followed him.

The tide was out, and the wet sand was soft under his trainers. Rusty was heading to the right, making for the flat rocks with crevices between them that were always full of sea water. He'd found a half-eaten hamburger there once, and never forgotten it.

Rusty wasn't born when Dad used to take them

for picnics on these rocks, Mick thought, him and Kate when they were small. He always made such an adventure of it, taking enough stuff for a week's safari, towels and a rug, spades, buckets, shrimping nets (though they never caught any shrimps), swimming costumes, radio 'to keep in touch with the outside world', lemonade, sandwiches, biscuits, bananas. The rocks had seemed so big then, and the gaps between them so wide, impossible to jump over. Great when a strong hand grabbed yours and swung you across as if you were flying.

Gran had said Bob was in heaven after it happened. She'd been quite sensible then, able to think about things like that. But it didn't help much. There were no postcards from heaven, no words to explain where he was and why. Nothing. No more laughs, no more daft pretending. 'You're all I've got,' Cathie said, hugging him. Time to grow up.

And now he was so grown up that Cathie didn't need him any more, and neither did anyone else. Kate was all right, she had Jake and the coming baby. *I'm expendable*, he thought. Maybe the fortune teller could see that in the cards.

Rusty yelped sharply.

'What's the matter?' Mick went to look, and the

dog struggled out of a deep cleft between the rocks, hopping on three legs and holding up a front paw.

'Show me.'

Rusty trustingly put his paw in Mick's hand. It was dripping with blood from a deep gash across one of the pads. *Glass*, Mick thought. The alkies quite often tossed an empty bottle over the railings to smash on the rocks below. But at least the dog was alive. The evil fate that hung around had not caused him to drown in some seaweedy pool or fall and break his neck. 'Come on,' he said, and started for home with Rusty limping at his side.

'You were down on the *rocks*? At *this* time of night?' Cathie stared at him, distraught. 'There's no lights along there, you could have been mugged or anything.'

Donald crouched down beside Rusty, who lay down and held all four paws in the air with his eyes rolling anxiously. Donald inspected the injury then said, 'I don't think there's any glass in it. Will I ring the vet?'

'It's half-past ten,' said Cathie. 'A bit much to disturb him at this time of night. And expensive.'

'D'you have a bandage or something?'

'Yes, of course.' She produced the First Aid box.

Donald ripped the blue wrapping off a bandage and said, 'Mick, can you hold his paw still?'

'Sure.'

Mick had to admit, Donald made a good job of it. He wrapped Rusty's paw in lint with some antiseptic cream on it then swathed it in cotton wool and bandaged it firmly, securing it with a safety pin. Rusty jumped to his feet as soon as he was released and ran round the kitchen floor, still holding up the injured paw. Then he sat down and panted expectantly.

'He wants a biscuit,' said Mick. 'He always has one after a walk.' He got a biscuit out of the packet – then thought of something. Where was Sheena? She'd been here when he went out, but he could see through the sitting-room door from where he stood, and she wasn't on the sofa any more.

Cathie read his thoughts. 'Sheena's in bed upstairs,' she said, not quite managing to meet his eye. 'She was tired, and we still had a lot of things to talk about.'

'Right,' said Mick. *So Sheena is staying the night*, he thought, *and so is her father presumably*. He wondered where Donald would be sleeping, and decided he'd rather not think about it.

When Mick came down to the kitchen in the morning, Cathie was sitting at the table alone, drinking tea and reading the paper. There was no sign of Donald or Sheena – or of Rusty, either.

'It's all right,' Cathie said, seeing his look of alarm. 'Don's taken him to the vet, just to get him checked over.'

Mick nodded. *Don*, he thought. Things had moved on, hadn't they. He glanced at his mother, but she didn't seem to notice. She was spreading another bit of toast with marmalade, and smiling.

Thirteen

The next day, school began again. On the first morning, a girl called Fiona Lee who had never spoken to Mick before came up and said, 'How awful about your fortune thing. Aren't you scared?' She had a couple of friends with her and they were both looking goggle-eyed and inclined to giggle.

'Not really,' said Mick, trying to sound cool. 'Load of rubbish, isn't it.' And he walked away under his private cloud of dread.

So much for Chloë's promise not to tell anyone, he thought. At break time he went to find her.

'I didn't!' she protested. 'I never said a word, honest.'

'Then how does Fiona Lee know?'

'Her mum works in the launderette,' said Chloë. 'She gets all the gossip in there.'

'S'pose so.' Mick hadn't thought about adults gossiping. It seemed a bit weird that any of them even knew, but Cathie had probably told various acquaintances, and people at the Centre could well have picked it up. Mick couldn't see Duncan as a gossiper, but Kate wouldn't mind talking about it, because she didn't believe in it. 'Sorry,' he said to Chloë. He'd been unfair to her.

'That's all right,' she said. 'Did you go and see the woman?'

'Yes,' said Mick. 'Wish I hadn't.'

'Was it awful?'

'The pits.' He couldn't go through the story, not even to Chloë. He was too sick of the whole thing, too sodden with dread and fear. He'd read somewhere that an animal will bite its own paw off if it's caught in a trap. Anything to be free. He felt like that now. He couldn't persuade himself that the trap wasn't real, and he'd do anything to get out of it.

'Well, I'm on your side,' said Chloë. 'You can fight it off, Mick, I know you can.'

'Thanks,' said Mick.

By lunchtime, Danny and Neil had got to hear about it as well. 'Why didn't you say?' Neil asked. 'I mean, we're your mates.'

'I know.' Perhaps he should have done, Mick thought. But they'd have turned it into a laugh, specially Danny. He could imagine the greeting in the morning – 'Hi – so the hex hasn't got you yet?' He ought to be able to laugh about it, he knew that. And he would, he really would, if it wasn't for this weight of dread in his stomach that made him feel vaguely sick all the time.

School somehow failed to make him feel any better. He couldn't concentrate or even feel much interested in what was going on, and when the final bell went he made a quick get-away and headed off across the bridge to the grassy hill and the ruined castle.

The hot days of summer had gone. He sat by the wall where he had sat that other time, when Rusty had panted beside him and he hadn't known what lay in wait. He rested his arms on his bent knees and put his head down, but he could find no peace. A gusty wind was blowing across the sea, and the sky was overcast. It wasn't warm.

All the same, he stayed there for quite a time. He wished he was still working at the Centre, where he had to watch what he was doing, and where it didn't seem so odd to be burdened with a thing that nobody else understood. They were all a bit like that, Duncan and Harry and the rest of them, coping as best they could with a pain in the brain that other people thought was stupid.

It crossed his mind that Cathie might be worrying, but he pushed the thought aside in a kind of weary anger. Cathie wasn't with him in this any more. She'd done the sensible thing and settled for what made her happy. Last night when he'd come in with Rusty and his cut paw, she'd protested about him going down on the rocks, but she wasn't frantic any more. She'd go on getting flutters of alarm but she'd moved away from it, and that was a good thing. She'd be all right.

Mick walked slowly down the hill and back into the town. He turned down Fisher Street, hoping Kate would be in.

She wasn't. Nobody answered when he rang the bell. He rapped on the door with his knuckles in case the bell wasn't working, but there was still silence.

He felt very alone, standing there in the empty street. He stared at the thistles and dandelions that grew in the patch of earth under the window. Kate had said she'd dig them up and plant some flowers. The walls were white, with a lot of spray-can graffiti. Very bare, no shelter. Anyone standing here was very visible. Something could look down from the sky and see him.

Mick thought of the awful TV pictures that had

shown a man and a boy in Palestine or somewhere, crouching against a white wall like this. The man was trying to shelter his son from gunmen. There was a dustbin by the wall, but that was no help, and neither was the man's outstretched hand or the words he was shouting, the gunmen shot the pair of them anyway. The boy fell sideways across his father's knees.

It knows where I am, Mick thought, alone against the white wall. There was no escape. Even in bed, wrapped in warmth and darkness, he could be seen. The thing could stop his heart when it chose.

He forced himself to move out on to the pavement again. There was a tight pain in his chest like when he was a little kid and cried sometimes, and a thin, high-pitched noise seemed to be going on somewhere in his head. A detached part of his mind wondered if he was going mad. People at the Centre said you didn't know it was happening, it was just that things got more and more awful. Next thing you knew, you were in a locked ward, getting injected with drugs to keep you calm. Sane people were supposed to be calm. *We were never calm*, he thought. When Bob got angry he was truly furious, and in between, he was like something in a play, smiling, raising a glass. *Your very good health.*

Mick knew he mustn't think about all that. It made the ache in his chest worse. He walked on, staring at each crack in the pavement, across Union Street, across the railway line, round the corner to the green. The sea was colourless, the sky heavy and grey. He came to the crazy golf with its faded blue and pink and yellow silly-shaped concrete ramps half overgrown with grass and dandelions, and stopped. Nobody cared for these weeds. Nobody planted them, they just grew, here and in front of Kate's flat, anywhere they could. If some huge disaster happened and the human race was wiped out, the dandelions would still grow.

It was such a small, bleak scrap of comfort that the pity of it shook him. Mick took a few further blundering steps, but the ache in his chest and throat rose into a buzzing fury behind his eyes, and he leaned against the wooden hut where they used to sell tickets in the summer, and wept.

A small child came and stared at him, its eyes as round as the dummy in its mouth. Mick rubbed his face on his sleeve, knowing the kid's mother would come after it at any moment, and turned away. He walked across to the railings and leaned his arms on them, shoulders hunched. The wind gradually dried his face. He kept his eyes

145

resolutely open, knowing that if he closed them, the tears would come again.

After a bit he stood back, feeling less wobbly. He pushed his hands into the pockets of his denim jacket and walked on. He was passing the glassed-in shelter (only most of its glass was plywood now because the kids had broken the windows) when a voice called him.

'Ah, Michael!'

Miss McIver, he thought. He'd know those genteel Edinburgh tones anywhere. There she was, doing her horrible crochet, with a magazine on her lap.

'Just home from school?' she enquired.

'That's right.' He went to walk past, but she held up a finger and said, 'Could I have a word?'

Reluctantly, Mick approached.

Miss McIver patted the bench beside her and said, 'Do sit down.' When he had done so, she looked at him from her watery blue eyes and said, 'I'm worried about your mother.'

Mick nearly said, *That makes two of us*, but decided not to. He watched the crochet hook dart in and out between the loops of black wool, and waited.

'I never gossip,' Miss McIver went on, 'but I am afraid the same cannot be said for Mrs Morris.

She told me an extraordinary tale about your mother visiting a so-called teller of fortunes.'

'Yes,' said Mick. There was no point in denying it.

'Devil worship.' Miss McIver pursed her lips and poked the little hook more fiercely in and out of the black wool.

Mick blinked. 'Um—'

'Your mother has been led astray by Satan, Michael. These wicked cards. The Devil's books. I spoke to her about it this morning, but she wouldn't listen. And that builder fellow she's taken up with was barely polite.' She shot Mick another glance. 'You are the only one who can make her see sense.'

This was all he needed, Mick thought – a lecture from a religious nutter. He knew Miss Em was a fervent church-goer, but she usually kept her views to herself.

'She is worried about your safety because of this ridiculous prediction,' Miss McIver went on. 'She cannot believe that God sees all things, both present and future. She has no faith.' A drip was gathering at the end of her nose and Mick watched it in fascination as the reproachful words continued. 'With such an attitude it is hardly surprising she is not in a state of grace, but you,

Michael, can show her the power of God.'

'Me? But how—'

'She is trying to keep you safe.' Miss McIver produced a lace-edged hanky and dabbed delicately at the drip. 'But that is arrogance, Michael. Only those who lack trust in the Lord would take it on themselves to do such a thing. Safety is in the hands of God, not of mere humans.'

'What am I supposed to do, then?'

'Take the risk,' Miss McIver said as if it was obvious. 'Do not let yourself be wrapped in cotton wool. Tell your mother she must not worry or attempt to keep you safe. When she sees that you walk unharmed through life's small dangers, she will stop believing in this prediction, which is the work of Satan. And so will you, Michael.' The pale blue eyes darted another fierce glance at him. 'You will be free.'

Nice idea, Mick thought. But a snag struck him. 'What if God wants me to die?'

'Then you must accept His will,' said Miss McIver. 'Faith casts out all fear.'

If he hadn't been feeling so detached and strange, Mick could have laughed. Miss Em's faith was no different from the fortune teller's when you came right down to it. They both believed something else was in charge and you had no choice about what happened.

'Put it to the test,' Miss McIver said. 'The Lord will not be found wanting.' She glanced at her watch and added, 'If you are going home, Michael, will you tell your mother I'll be in shortly? I am a little late, but tea is seldom on time these days.'

'I'll tell her,' said Mick. He stood up. 'Nice talking to you.' *Always be polite to the guests.*

Miss McIver, busy again with her crochet, nodded but did not answer. *And remember,* Bob used to say, *the guests don't have to be polite to you.*

Mick paused automatically at the road's edge to let a car go by. Perhaps Miss Em would disapprove of that. Should he have hurled himself in front of the vehicle so as to give God a chance to rescue him? If so, tough. Even God couldn't stop a car doing forty miles an hour along this straight bit. *Put it to the test.* But it had to be a fair test.

He went into the kitchen and Rusty got out of his basket and came towards him with wagging tail. The injured paw was encased in a waterproof dressing, and Rusty didn't seem to mind putting his weight on it today. It made a light, tapping noise on the floor as he capered round Mick in welcome.

'Come on, then, Peg-leg,' Mick said. He went up to his room with the dog at his heels, and sat on his bed. Rusty managed to scramble up and lie beside him, panting happily, and Mick stroked him. It was the best feeling he'd had all day, the rough fur under his hand. He swung his feet up from the floor and lay back with his head on the pillow.

Put it to the test, he thought again. All very well, but how? If there really was something in charge – God, or fate, or whatever you called it – there was never any way of getting a straight look at it. The thing was always just out of his sight, like the game of grandmother's footsteps they used to play as kids, where one person stood facing the wall while the others crept up behind him. He could turn at any time, and if he saw anyone moving, they had to go back to the start. But each time he looked round, the nearest one was a little closer, and he knew he'd be pounced on one of these times when he looked away.

Cathie tapped at the door with light fingertips, then put her head round. 'Can I come in?'

'Sure.' Mick sat up.

His mother looked at him then frowned a little. 'Are you all right? Is your leg sore?'

'No, it's OK.'

'Oh, good.' She sat down beside him and took a deep breath. 'Mickey, I want to ask you something. Would you mind a lot if Don and I – what I mean is, if he moved in here? And Sheena. You don't have to say right away,' she rushed on. 'I want you to have time to think about it.'

Mick didn't need time to think, only to decide what to say. He'd known it was going to happen. They'd both known. Cathie was still talking.

'It would be so much handier. If you decide to take up Don's offer of working with him, you'd both be here, it's just easier for everyone. And so much cheaper, if he sells his house. Sheena could have Kate's room,' she went on. 'Not that we're short of space, but the business might pick up a bit with two of us working, and then we'd need all the guest rooms. Don's got plans to advertise. He says he'll do the kitchen up this winter, get it to Tourist Board standard ready for next season.' She was babbling in her anxiety, but then she ran out of words. 'It's just – you know, the whole thing.' She looked at him anxiously.

Mick shrugged. 'It doesn't make any difference,' he said. If the rest of the prediction was going to come true, then it would. Or it wouldn't. *I can't bear this much longer*, he thought.

'Oh, you are a darling,' Cathie said. She gave his hand a little squeeze. 'I was afraid you and Don were never going to get on at first, but it's different now, isn't it? He really likes you, you know.'

'Yes,' Mick heard himself say. He felt as distant from himself as he had when he left the fortune teller's flat. He was looking down as if from some high place at himself and his mother, sitting on the bed with the dog between them. Like a security camera in a shop, he thought with vague interest, or someone newly dead, looking back on what his life has been. He wondered if he should try to tell Cathie what it was like to seem so far away, but decided not to. She'd probably freak out. He made a big effort to concentrate.

'When are they moving in?' he asked, cutting across what Cathie was saying.

She looked just a shade guilty. 'We thought in the next day or two, if you're sure you're all right about it.'

'Yes,' Mick said again. Then he added in remote interest, 'What if I hadn't been?'

'Well – we'd have waited, of course. Given it more time.'

Mick smiled. It was very simple, he thought. Given enough time, fate would solve all problems.

Didn't Cathie see what she was saying? She and Don would wait, and one day Mick either wouldn't mind or he wouldn't be here.

From his great distance, he saw Cathie reach across the dog and take her son's hand, and wondered in a detached sort of way why the boy did not lean forward and kiss her.

Fourteen

'Time you were off to bed, Sheena,' said Donald the next night.

It hadn't taken them long to move in, Mick thought. A day of bustling about with the van and here they were, looking as if they'd never lived anywhere else. The rest of their stuff was coming tomorrow. 'I'll take Rusty out,' he said.

'Just into the garden,' Cathie warned. 'The vet said no walks for the next few days.'

Donald patted the dog and said, 'We'll soon have you better.'

He's not your dog, Mick thought. He stood up and whistled, and Rusty pattered towards him, tail wagging.

'Now, you won't take him far, will you, Mickey?' Cathie sounded as if she didn't quite trust him not to disappear for hours. She might be right.

'No,' said Mick. The dog would be back within five minutes.

When Rusty had relieved himself against one of the washing-line poles in the back garden, Mick pushed him gently back through the kitchen door. 'Sorry,' he said. Then he walked on down the drive and across the road. It was getting dark, and a fine smirr of rain was blowing in from the sea. Mick wished he'd brought a jacket, but he wasn't going back now. He half closed his eyes against the dampness in the wind. Better out here than in the stuffy room with everyone smiling at each other.

He followed the familiar route across the green and rounded the corner by the pub, then crossed the railway line. The lighthouse beam was already flashing. It swept the sky behind the warehouse buildings, gave way to the half-darkness then swept again, two seconds on, two seconds off.

A part of Mick's mind still felt strangely distant. *There must have been a lot of shipwrecks in the days before lighthouses*, it observed. He'd been down here in the winter sometimes, watching while the waves crashed against the wall and came bursting over the top of it, falling into the car park with a hiss and rattle of spray. It was a risky job at the best of times, steering through the narrow entrance to the harbour. Sea captains didn't like risk. They fought it with everything they'd got, radar, echo-sounders, careful men on the bridge and in the engine room, years of long experience.

I hate experience, Mick's mind said to him. He was fed up with the endless procession of things that kept on happening, dull and boring or else spiked with fear. He wouldn't care if it all stopped.

Quite suddenly, he knew what he was going to do. *Yes, of course.* He could see himself standing there, quite small compared with the wall's height and the open sweep of the sea. *Take the risk.* But the thought of it made his heart thump with terror.

He was still walking. The dock was on his right, lit with orange sodium lit behind its high iron fence. The oblong shapes of lorry containers stood there, waiting to be loaded on the Irish ferry, and a sea of blue plastic covered bale upon bale of peat, shipped in from Belfast. *How strange, to be digging up Ireland and sending it away.* But it wasn't his problem. He was crossing the unlit car park now. Climbing the steps to the wall, walking along it.

Not many cars down there tonight. Nobody driving around like crazy.

He'd never know what happened. *What's it like, Dad, being dead?*

No reply, of course. A single car drove into the car park but it stopped and its lights went out. Not going anywhere.

Mick walked a few paces further, then came to a halt. The wash of the sea slopping against the wall below him was loud in his ears and the two-second swing of the light made him feel almost dizzy. He put his hands on the stone parapet and looked down. It was odd to feel so calm although he was sick with fear. The sea covered the rocks even when it fell away between each surge of the tide, but he couldn't be sure how much depth there was.

That makes it fair. Not like stepping in front of a car that couldn't stop. This way, there was a chance that he'd hit one of the deep gaps between the rocks. He was a strong swimmer. If the dive didn't kill him, with any luck he'd make it past the lighthouse and in through the mouth of the harbour. He could see himself crawling up the slipway, sodden and exhausted – yes, the little figure looked barely able to move.

His lungs were bucking like frightened rabbits in the cage of his chest, and he couldn't breathe properly, and yet he looked down with compassion on Mick Finn, who stood on the wall with the soft rain blowing in his face. He was easing his feet out of his trainers, the left then the right. He wanted to keep his socks on because they were warm and comforting. *The boy will swim better without them*. He bent down and took them off.

The stone of the parapet wasn't as cold as he'd expected. He crouched there, steadying himself with his fingertips on either side of him. He would have to jump well out. He raised his head, looking beyond the swirling water below him to the horizon where a streak of light remained. *Better stand up*. He persuaded his legs to straighten, then shuffled forward a little so his toes could grip the edge of the stone. He dragged some breath into his jibbing, fluttering lungs and raised his arms. The lighthouse beam swung across him one last time.

'*MICK*!'

The shout jolted like an electric shock through Mick's outstretched fingers and flexed, trembling knees. He gasped and thought he was inhaling sea water, but it was rain and spray, and he was still standing on the terrible edge, in a nightmare that hadn't stopped.

'MICK! For God's sake, what are you doing?'

In his confusion, Mick didn't know if the voice came from the land or the sky. He took a small step back and the lighthouse beam caught him like a fly. He almost lost his balance, and in that second his whole self, both the watcher and the trembling, terrified body, came together in the panic that he might fall.

It was over. He was desperate to stay alive. Water was running down his face, some of it rain and some of it salty and warm.

Running footsteps came towards him. 'Hang on, I'm coming, hang on, Mick, stay where you are!' Arms were flung round him, he was lifted down, hugged close in a soft, smoky-smelling jersey. 'God's sake, boy, what were you thinking of?' It was Jake.

Mick was eight years old again, crying like a kid who's had the fright of his life. Jake held him tightly for a long time, then he said, 'Let's get off this bloody wall.'

He handed Mick his socks, and Mick pulled them on over his wet feet. Jake was tugging at the laces of the kicked-off trainers.

'I'll do it,' Mick said, though he was terribly cold now and his teeth were chattering.

Jake took no notice. He crouched and offered a shoe for Mick to step into, then tied it firmly. 'Other one,' he ordered, and Mick obediently changed feet. There was nothing in the sky but sweet rain. No threat. He cried all over again with the relief of it.

'Put this on.' Jake had hauled his sweater off and was slipping it over Mick's head. 'Arms up.'

Mick tried to say he was OK, but there was wool over his face and his hands were being pushed into warm sleeves.

'Come on,' said Jake, and took his hand.

Mick released himself when they'd gone down the steps and were crossing the car park. He noticed absently that the car which had driven in had gone now. He couldn't understand why the miracle of Jake's arrival had happened. 'What made you come?' he asked.

Jake shrugged, or it could have been that he was cold without his sweater. 'Said I'd meet a guy down here,' he said. 'To buy some stuff off him. Where are we going – your place or mine?'

'Yours,' said Mick. 'Please.'

Kate was ironing. 'Hi, Mick,' she said casually. Then she looked at him again. 'You all right?'

'He hit a bit of a crisis,' Jake said. 'I think we both need some hot chocolate.' And he went off to make some.

Kate unplugged the iron and stood it in the fireplace beside the electric fire. Then she sat down beside Mick on the sofa and said, 'Tell me what happened.'

The story upset her much more than he'd expected. She put her hands over her mouth in a long gasp of horror. 'Mick, you cuckoo!' Her eyes were bright with tears. 'What would I do without you?'

He'd never thought Kate would say that. She had Jake and the flat, didn't she, not to mention the baby that was going to be born. 'But you're all right,' he said.

Kate shook her head impatiently. 'You don't love people because you *need* them. Can't you see? You love them for being themselves.' She reached forward and slid her hand round the back of his neck. 'You great idiot,' she said gently.

The warmth of the hot chocolate spread through Mick to his fingers and toes, and he began to feel sleepy.

'I'd better phone Mum,' said Kate. 'Tell her where you are.'

He had a moment's alarm. 'Don't say anything about—'

'Course I won't. You'll have to tell her, though, Mick, at some point. And about going to see the fortune woman, the whole thing. She's not a baby, she ought to know.'

'Suppose so.'

Kate picked up the phone and dialled. She sounded light and easy as she spoke to Cathie. 'No, he's fine, just sleepy. OK if he stays here tonight? We'll drop him back in time for school in the morning . . . Sure . . . Yes, I will. Bye.'

'Was she all right?'

'Yes, seemed almost chirpy. A bit cross, but not frantic. She sent you her love.'

Perhaps she knew it was over as well, Mick thought. He turned on his side, nestling more comfortably into the cushions.

'I'll get a blanket,' said Kate, and went to look for one.

Jake sat down beside Mick in her place. 'I found this, by the way,' he said. He was opening a flat, black box with scuffed corners. 'Clarinet. Told you I had one.'

Mick propped himself on his elbow and looked at the glossy black sections of the instrument, lying in their padded nest. Cautiously, he touched the bright metal rings and levers, wondering if he could really get to understand how they worked. 'I'll never do it,' he said, and yet the hope was there.

'Yes, you will,' said Jake. 'These reeds will be a bit hard for a beginner, but I'll rub a couple down a bit.'

The words meant nothing to Mick, but he smiled and said, 'Great.'

Jake closed the box and clicked the catches into place. 'Tomorrow,' he said.

Mick lay down again. Sleep was overwhelming him like a soft sea in which nobody drowned. He was barely aware of a rug being tucked round him, or of his trainers being unlaced and taken off, for the second time that evening.

He slept more soundly than he had done for weeks. In the morning, Kate woke him in time for cornflakes and toast, and Jake said he'd run him home.

Mick wouldn't let him. It was no distance, and anyway, he wanted to be outside on his own, in the new emptiness of the sky.

'Don't forget about telling Mum,' Kate said on the doorstep. 'If you don't, I will.'

'No need to come the heavy,' said Mick. 'I'll tell her. And – thanks for everything.'

Kate smiled. 'Just don't make it a habit,' she said.

The clouds had blown away in the night, and the air was sharp and clear. The sea sparkled in the morning sun and gulls barked at each other in their raucous way, perching on the high lamp-posts to drop rude white sploshes on the pavement below. It was all very good.

Mick couldn't think clearly yet about what had happened. Miss Em would no doubt claim that God had stepped in, but it could equally be pure chance that Jake had been there, doing an illegal little deal, probably with the driver of the car that had come in and switched its lights off. Perhaps chance *was* God. Either way, it was a mystery, but not one that you had to be afraid of.

He barged into the kitchen with just enough time to change out of Jake's sweater into a clean sweatshirt and stick a fresh dressing on his burned leg. Cathie wanted to know why he'd gone off out last night without a word to anyone, but Mick just picked up his school bag and said, 'Can't stop now, I'll be late. I'll tell you about it after school, OK?'

'Well – OK,' said Cathie. And he gave her a quick kiss then went out.

The school day was splendidly normal. Miss Armitage gave Mick a telling-off for not having done his Maths homework, but he dealt with it easily. 'Something came up,' he told her, and gave her what he thought of as his Social Services look, confidential and a bit embarrassed. 'To do with the family.' It wasn't a thing you could use often, otherwise they really would send a social worker round, but it was great in emergencies.

'Oh.' Miss Armitage looked worried. 'Well – can you get it done over the weekend? I don't want you getting behind.'

'No problem,' said Mick. Neil and Danny grinned at him, looking interested. They knew something had changed.

At break time he told them about Jake's offer to teach him the clarinet, and Neil looked puzzled. 'Never knew you were interested,' he said. Danny said his dad was great on the tin whistle, and an argument started about whether a whistle and a clarinet were the same sort of thing. Mick didn't know, but it gave him a good feeling inside to think he soon would.

There was football practice after school. Mick never went – he wasn't much good at football. He started out for home on his own, but halfway down Union Street Chloë caught him up.

'You all right?' she asked.

'Absolutely fine.'

'Oh, good.' She looked at him with curiosity. 'Has something happened? You seem sort of different.'

'It's just – I don't feel scared any more.' One day he'd tell her what happened, but not right now. He wasn't quite used to it yet.

'Terrific,' said Chloë. 'How weird, though. Did you suddenly think, "I don't believe it"?'

'Not really. It went away, that's all. It isn't there any more.'

There was a crowd of people on the pavement ahead of them. A police car had pulled up with its blue light flashing.

'Oh, no,' said Chloë. 'There's been an accident.'

As they got closer, Mick saw that the crowd was clustered round the betting shop. A wild certainty grabbed him, but he pushed it away. *No. Can't be.*

Mrs Morris was among the people, and she spotted Mick and pushed her way towards him. Her face was pink with excitement and her woolly hat was askew. 'Can you believe it!' she said. 'I can't wait to tell your mother.'

'Tell her what?' But he knew, he knew.

'The woman she went to see. The fortune teller. Lying dead up there since last night, can you imagine. Her friend found her – that man over there with the moustache. He had a key to the flat. Let himself in this afternoon and there she was. Gone.'

166

'How do you know she died last night?' Mick demanded.

'There was a woman from the press here, interviewing people. She had a tape recorder. The police officer told her.'

'What *time*?'

Mrs Morris looked surprised at his urgency. 'About ten, they think. There'll have to be an autopsy, of course.'

She was enjoying this, Mick thought. And why not? It would give her something to talk about for weeks. His own feelings were too scattered and astonished to get hold of. The fortune teller could have died just as he was crouched on the wall trying to will his legs to straighten and his fingertips to leave their contact with the stone. *There will be a death*, old Beth had said. An ambulance pulled up.

Chloë was looking stunned. 'No wonder you thought it had gone away,' she said.

Mick didn't answer. Verity Rose had been alive and real. Black eyes, fancy glasses, orange hair, a cold lunch on the table. He wouldn't have wished her dead. Maybe she had dealt the cards for herself in the evenings sometimes. Maybe she, too, was frightened. What if she'd seen a death forecast again and again, and tried to push away

167

the knowledge that it was her own? When Cathie turned up, fitting what the cards said so exactly, what a relief it would have been. How wonderful to hand it on to someone else.

Not that she should have been bothered. *Look forward with joy* ... She was sure she'd be born again. Mick had an absurd vision of a baby with frizzy orange hair and glasses with flyaway sides. *Best of luck*, he thought. And if it wasn't like that at all, if it was just the end, then she wouldn't know. He felt strangely sorry for Verity Rose in spite of everything. The man with a moustache who had the key to her flat was standing with a couple of policemen, looking wooden-faced and not particularly upset. Mrs Morris had given up trying to get any sense out of Mick and was talking to Chloë instead.

Donald's van stopped on the other side of the road, and Donald got out of it and came across to Mick. 'What's going on?' he asked.

'It's the fortune teller. She's dead.'

'Good grief.'

Chloë, at Mick's side, said, 'See you tomorrow,' then walked on. Mrs Em had burst into a fresh spate of information, delighted to find someone who didn't know.

Donald only half listened. His eyes kept

returning to Mick as the excited words ran on, and after a few minutes he gave a sideways movement of the head that invited him to come over to the van. Mick followed him across the road. This was probably going to be a telling-off about going out last night and not coming back, he thought.

'I'll have to go,' Donald said, 'they've a freezer broken down at the Co-op.' He frowned, though not in annoyance. 'See, Mick, I'm no' much good with words, but there's things we've to sort out.'

'I'm sorry about last night,' said Mick – but Donald shook his head.

'It's more than that.' He took a deep breath. 'I'll never be like your dad, I know that. I'm a bit short on charisma. I don't get what people mean unless they say.' His sticking-out ears were very pink. 'So if there's times you think I ought to understand something and I don't, you'll just have to tell me. That's, if you want to.'

Mick nodded. He wasn't much good with words, either. 'Yes,' he said. He couldn't remember when a grown-up person had said anything as straight as that. 'Yes, I will.' Then he added, 'Thanks.'

Donald got into the van then said through the open window, 'Can't stop now, they'll have water all over the floor. But we'll give it a go, eh?'

'Yes,' Mick said again. And Donald drove off.

'Stand clear now.'

'Over there, madam, if you please.'

The police were herding people behind barriers, leaving a space outside the doorway by the betting shop. Mick watched from across the road as the ambulance men brought out a stretcher with a burden on it that was completely covered by a firmly-strapped dark green sheet. The woman called Verity Rose wasn't a person any more, she had turned into a parcel, something to be dealt with and disposed of. He turned away.

Over the railway line, round the corner, out on the green. The sea was as blue and innocent as a baby's eye, the sun lower in the sky now than it had been. September. The Council would be along with a truck before long, to dig up all the plants in the flowerbeds, then there would be bare earth until next spring, when they'd plant some new ones. Have another shot at poshing the place up. The years went round and round and nobody knew how it worked, but it didn't matter.

This winter, Mick thought, he really would catch the moment when the lighthouse shone out for the first time. With any luck.

DEAR DEL

Alison Prince

'It's not often you know you're happy, but at that moment, sitting with my arms around my knees and tasting the saltiness of my skin, I felt that, no matter what happened afterwards, I would remember this for ever . . .'

Before Della arrives to stay with her on the remote scottish island where she lives, Fran builds her up to be the best mate she's been longing for since she and her family moved from lively London to boring Broray. Fran and Del are going to have such a laugh; swimming, climbing, exploring the island. Fran can't wait.

But Della's arrival is a disappointment, to say the least. She's 'Del', not Della, and she's downright rude and unfriendly. She makes Fran feel like a stupid kid. A whole *week* with this nightmare? Fran is counting the days . . .

BIRD BOY

Alison Prince

'. . . *I could never make the sound of human words, Conan. They said I was mad. But neither could I sing as the birds do, only clatter and croak like a crow.'*

'*What happened?' Con asked, with his heart thudding. 'Tell me.'*

Con and his family have moved to a crumbling house deep in the Suffolk countryside. They have big plans for the future, but instead they find themselves caught up in the past, in a tragedy so tightly entwined with Con's own family that it holds them all helpless. Until its memory can be put to rest.

The bird boy is waiting . . .

WALLISCOTE PRIMARY
SCHOOL
WALLISCOTE ROAD
WESTON-SUPER-MARE
BS23 1UY 01934-621924